SET APART
FROM THE
REST

Unexpected Truth

J.B. Morales

WESTBOW·
PRESS
A DIVISION OF THOMAS NELSON
& ZONDERVAN

WestBow Press books may be ordered through booksellers or by contacting:

WestBow Press
A Division of Thomas Nelson & Zondervan
1663 Liberty Drive
Bloomington, IN 47403
www.westbowpress.com
1 (866) 928-1240

Scripture taken from the New King James Version. Copyright 1979, 1980, 1982 by Thomas Nelson, inc. Used by permission. All rights reserved.

Scriptures taken from the Holy Bible, New International Version®, NIV®. Copyright © 1973, 1978, 1984, 2011 by Biblica, Inc.™ Used by permission of Zondervan. All rights reserved worldwide. www.zondervan.com The "NIV" and "New International Version" are trademarks registered in the United States Patent and Trademark Office by Biblica, Inc.™ All rights reserved.

ISBN: 978-1-4908-6233-0 (sc)
ISBN: 978-1-4908-6234-7 (hc)
ISBN: 978-1-4908-6232-3 (e)

Library of Congress Control Number: 2014921561

Printed in the United States of America.

WestBow Press rev. date: 12/22/2014

Prologue

God gave the ending of the story at the beginning. God spoke this into existence and made it known to man. The Scriptures, inspired by God, were made available to all so they may know the truth. It is sad to say that many disregard the truth and hide under a veil of false truth. This story is inspired by the Holy Spirit. Woe to anyone who reads this and disregards it. You know the truth, but do you know how it leads to the ending?

Jim stood at the window and looked out at the dreary storm. The storm continued to beat against the old window pane. He inhaled deeply and then sighed. His best friends were here together in this hospital room. One was in a coma and looked like he was on his deathbed. No one knew what strength George was using to cling to life. Jim and his other two friends, Kyle and James, thought about how George had fallen so far off the reservation, and Jim continued to subdue those painful memories. He pulled his hands from his pockets and placed them on the window sill.

Jim looked out of the window at the storm and said, "During the course of my life, I have heard of the living Word of God. I have heard of visions and dreams and supernatural things. My story begins with trials, triumphs, and vivid dreams. These dreams have made me dread my slumber and given me such fear. I have pleaded with my conscience to live upright with moral standards. Unfortunately, the world and its system are corrupt and seek to destroy us on a daily basis. I don't know what will come of these stories, but the Holy Spirit has given me this work to complete. I heard the Holy Spirit tell me, 'Hear the truth and wisdom. Many seek it, even to the point of desolation.'" While staring at the beating rain he thought of how this journey had begun. He wondered about George's internal struggles for his friend to turn so far against him as well as God.

"Why does he have so much hatred toward everyone?" asked Kyle.

Jim did not reply; he was lost in his thoughts. He racked his memory for the origin of George's struggle. He tried to remember if he had done anything that directly affected George's decision. And then he remembered.

It all began one night with a dream.

1

Jim was lying in his bed, uncomfortably tossing and turning. The room was devoid of light, except for the occasional gleam of a headlight from a passing car. He breathed deeply, thinking of whether or not to count imaginary sheep and wondering who thought of sheep jumping over a fence in the first place.

It seemed to take hours to calm his mind. Jim tried every method that he could think of. He loved to sleep but dreaded the realistic dreams that haunted him. He finally drifted off and awoke in a dream. "I'm back home, back when I was several years younger," he said.

He knew that he was in middle school and thought about a girl named Christie. During his youth, he'd had a crush on Christie. From the day he met her in kindergarten, even until now, he liked her. One day, she told him that she wanted to meet with him at the mall. He constantly replayed the conversation in his head. He promised her that he would be there at six that evening.

His hair was still in a careless bed-head mode, and his clothes seemed like they would be better used for lawn work. They were mismatched and dingy from years of wear. He browsed through his closet and found his last clean shirt. The shirt also was dingy and faded, but at least it was clean. The pants that he chose were faded too. He slid his feet into a black pair of shoes as if they were house slippers. Then he begged his dad to take him to the mall, and luckily, this time his dad seemed in a good mood. The car ride to the mall was shorter than he remembered.

Walking briskly, he headed straight for the escalator where he was to meet Christie—but she was nowhere to be found. He presumed she had gone to the food court to hang out. He gave a brief sigh of disappointment but continued to walk around. As he walked, he passed an elegant jewelry store and looked in the store window to admire the beautiful jewelry. White gold captured his attention; he was fascinated by its pure innocence. He knew that he couldn't afford it; after all, his savings from his allowance was not that much.

Unable to find Christie, he leaned against the wall in a moment of aggravation. Suddenly, his back and shoulders began to vibrate as his knees buckled beneath him. Against all reason, the walls and floors began to shake, and glass shattered from the ceiling. He thought an earthquake was happening, but he was nowhere in the geographical location for one to occur.

A frail woman with a cane lost her footing and collapsed, and all around Jim, people were screaming. Their howls echoed against the walls as panic set in. The lights flickered and then went out, plunging the mall into what seemed like an empty oblivion. Jim felt lost in the chaos—and then the emergency lights flickered, giving false hope.

Everyone rushed toward the exit, but then an intense high-pitched whistle reverberated through the corridors. The whistle seemed to penetrate Jim's very being, to the depths of his soul. At that moment, concrete and glass came crashing down from the ceiling, like boulders and daggers, killing those who were unfortunate to be in the path. Even though he was gripped by agonizing fear, Jim looked around—and he saw glowing rocks scattered among the glass and concrete boulders. The rocks were not ordinary and had an immense heat. As Jim looked to the sky, he observed balls of light—a shower of meteors—crashing through the atmosphere and colliding with the terrain.

Being on the second floor of the mall was not good for anyone. When the meteors fell, the impact caused the second floor to collapse and created a giant slide to the ground floor. At the base of this slide were molten steel and flickering flames. A fire spread across the floor from the intense heat and caused the area to ignite an inferno.

People fell onto this makeshift slide. They clawed with all their might to stay on solid ground. Some lost fingernails as gravity pulled them down to the pit. Terrified screams filled the air, creating a symphony of hopelessness. Jim immediately raced for the emergency exit. Sweat saturated his clothes, and he gasped for air. Through the intense heat and heavy smoke, he tried to follow the emergency exit signs that remained intact. The floor violently shook again and twisted as if it were a piece of rubber. The mall building made a grotesque whining sound, and Jim feared that the infrastructure was about to give. Just as Jim made it into the doorway of the stairwell, the floor crumbled, and he'd just made it through the door when the ceiling started to fall. Dust, coughs, and screams polluted the air. He had to move quickly, as the meteors were still falling to the ground with immense force. He made a dash for the grass near the parking lot. Most of the sidewalk near the grassy area had been broken up by various pieces of meteorites. The ground looked like a terrible construction site.

From a distance, Jim noticed a mob running toward the people who were exiting the mall. The mob began violently attacking and murdering anyone who exited the mall. Blood spattered the area as they were viciously attacked. Those who were not attacked dropped to their knees as they gasped for air. With their last breath, they begged for mercy but found none. The attackers gave no indication why they were harming and killing everyone. They laughed and mocked their victims and sounded as if they made a game of their actions.

Jim thought the faces of the attackers appeared normal. When he looked more closely, though, he could see that they wore masks. The masks were transparent and visible at the same time. The masks appeared ominous, resembling a cat with horns. One group of people had white masks and the other had gold masks.

Tears streamed down Jim's cheeks as the gruesome onslaught continued. He had to remain vigilant and determined if he wanted to escape with his life. He ran as fast as he could from the parking lot. He got a quarter of a mile down the street when he saw a swarm of giant bees. They were about the size of volleyballs and were wearing battle armor. He decided to run through the nearby forest and managed to run about three miles down the road when he found a group of people.

With caution, he examined them and began a slow approach. He wanted more time to carefully consider his options and determine if he could trust this group. He looked behind him and noticed the giant bees making their way toward him, so he decided to introduce himself to the group. The group finally noticed him and frantically waved, urging him to hurry. The air vibrated as the wings of the bees fluttered and made gusts of wind. He made it to the group as they were ducking into a sewer manhole. Jim was the last one in the manhole. He moved the extremely heavy manhole cover over his head. He did this with the surge of adrenaline that was pumping in his body as the giant bees passed over him.

Exhausted and confused, Jim attempted to make sense of things. His body ached from cuts and bruises. Now that he was safe, his adrenaline surge wore off. Fatigue began to set in his muscles like tar. An array of emotions plagued his soul, and he wanted to drift off to sleep. He thought of how alone he felt, now that he was separated from his family. As terrible as it was to stand in a sewer, it was worse to think about sleeping in one. He was relieved that it at least provided safety and cover from the chaos above.

Each person in the group took turns standing watch, with each watch lasting about four hours. During the shift, Jim leaned his head against the wall and let the sounds of the world fade away. While attempting to rest his mind, he thought about Christie and his family. When the shift ended, he lay in a makeshift bed. His eyes closed slowly until he finally drifted into sleep.

The next day, the members of the makeshift group attempted to search for families, friends, and loved ones. None of Jim's family was to be found. The group of people now consisted of thirty-four mismatched individuals. Each person had been separated from his or her friends and loved ones. When the disaster and chaos set in, they each had developed a fight-or-flight mind-set. They chose flight and ran as fast and as hard as they could from the chaos. Once they gained mental clarity, they paused and searched for shelter. This group found one another and agreed to watch for the safety of one another.

Later that day, Jim learned that the situation at the mall was a worldwide event. He could only wonder what had happened to Christie and to his family. He also wondered what had caused the chaotic night he had just endured.

The remaining individuals learned that a new world government had been established but not out of the United Nations. The United Nations had been destroyed during a world peace meeting the previous day. News officials had placed the blame on terrorist cells, natural phenomena, and global warming. The economy had a makeover, as all the currency had to become one universal currency. The person who masterminded this currency event was considered and agreed by all to be the wisest man alive. The group never caught his name or saw his face; they simply went into hiding for fear of their lives.

Rumors began to circulate that this leader had been placed in the position of ultimate authority. The check-and-balance system was disregarded, as he claimed it was his divine right to rule. Within a short time, everyone was required to register and implant a biometric chip in their forehead or right hand. The biometric chip was no bigger than a grain of rice and was highly sophisticated. The biometric chip contained any personal identifying information and also could track a person's health as well as his or her location. The government's new system was flawless and worked like a well-oiled machine. Jim had read about situations like this in the Bible and only could presume this was the end of days.

The group decided to create a buddy system in which they were to pair with another member at all times. Everyone in the group drew random sticks to pair up as partners. Jim was paired up with a girl named Leanne Dickinson. Leanne was roughly five foot four, with light brown frizzy hair. She had naturally long eyelashes and a thin upper lip. She was as perfect a person for a Jim as any other person. After being cooped up for so many hours, he just wanted to get away in the fresh air.

Their current predicament of hiding was like a spiral staircase that wound into the abyss. Leanne wanted a moment to herself, just a moment of fresh air. She made her way through the tunnel and navigated her way to a ladder. It felt like an eternity since they'd been outside the tunnels. She persuaded Jim to move the manhole cover. The crisp air funneled down and hit Jim's oily forehead like a shotgun. An immense amount of energy surged from his lungs to his legs. He used all his might to refrain from jumping with glee.

Jim's stomach began to churn from the excitement that was building. Leanne looked around to ensure that the coast was clear and then moved topside. He was ecstatic to finally get fresh air. Jim climbed topside and felt as if he were a nervous animal out of his habitat. He noticed blinding lights about two hundred yards ahead of them. His short time while spent in the sewer made his eyesight keen, like a hawk, and dulled his sense of smell. Leanne's gaze was fixed on something that he couldn't understand. He stood to her left and turned his head, attempting to understand why she was staring at a phone booth.

It finally came to him in a rush of information. It felt like his brain was a computer that was downloading information. It finally came crashing down on him like a sledgehammer that he had been out of sync with reality. The world had definitely changed. What used to be a crowded city was now leveled with dirt and tree bark everywhere, save for a phone booth. The phone booth that she was staring at was blinking. This is what disturbed him the most. The phone booth flickered on. There was an electronic sign that was attached to the phone booth that read, "Leanne and Jim, you have a phone call." It was as if Leanne was a brainwashed zombie; she kept walking toward the phone booth. Jim knew it was his duty not to leave or forsake his partner. Doing so would cause Jim to be an outcast from the safety that the group provided.

Leanne stepped inside the phone booth and picked up the phone. No sooner than she had done so than her eyes began to fill with tears that slowly fell across her cheeks.

"What's going on?" Jim asked. Leanne refused to say anything, but she handed him the phone. When Jim put the phone to his ear, worried over what he'd hear, there was a ten-second pause that seemed endless, and then a man's voice spoke from the other end of the phone. A knot formed in Jim's stomach as a stern voice told him, "It is time to leave." No sooner did the voice finish speaking than the phone booth fell lifeless. Once again, Jim was surrounded by darkness; there was not even a star in the sky.

He told Leanne what the voice had said. They decided to return to the sewer and warn the group. The group decided to vacate the safe house and tunnels. Jim saw that some of the members of the group wanted to collect personal items. "There isn't much time, we have to go!" exclaimed Jim. The group heard the urgency in his voice and knew that he was serious. They all went to the manhole that Jim and Leanne came from. Jim was the last person to make it topside. Several police vehicles pulled up. The group, filled with fear, began running in different directions; Jim ran with Leanne. The police officers got out of their vehicles and began restraining everyone they caught. As Jim ran, he heard muffled screams, and the wind whistling across his ears. Jim thought he and Leanne were going to escape. He discovered that he and Leanne were spotted by a rookie police officer, and thus the chase began. They ran for about two miles until they reached an apartment complex. They ran past a curb and with a set of brown poles. It turned out that the poles read and searched for biometric chips. If a person passed by the poles and did not have a chip, the poles would sound an alarm. The machines finished scanning them, and a great and loud alarm sounded.

As they ran up the stairs of one of the buildings in the complex, Jim and Leanne were joined by a group of strangers, and they all ran to an apartment on the left. Another group ran to the apartment on the right. As soon as Jim closed the door, he heard footsteps running up the stairs, followed by the sound of dogs barking out of control. Jim knew that it had to be the police that was pursuing them. Jim braced himself against the door as he heard someone break down the other door. He heard the group from the other apartment yelling that it was the police. After the brief pleading, Jim heard gunshots. The police didn't waste a second before they attempted to breakdown the door that Jim was guarding. Every time they hit the door, Jim was nearly knocked back from the amount of brute force they used.

The police finally managed to crack and destroy the top right corner of the door. Jim heard something thrown in the door, followed by another drop and crack. A loud bang occurred, followed by smoke that put everyone's senses in disarray. Jim fell to the ground, and the police broke in and fired at everyone they saw. It was by the grace of a miracle that they did not see Jim. He was curled up against the wall and had lost all ability to move.

The police were behind him now, looking for any survivors. His strength returned as he jumped to his feet with anger. Adrenaline rushed through his body and tears trickled down from his eyes. There was no longer any sound, neither cries nor footsteps behind him. He stopped dead in his tracks as his surroundings faded. There was an eerie and malevolent laugh from above. After the laughter, a loud, ominous sound said, "Behold! He has finally arrived and is in power." Jim lifted his head and saw a man overshadowing everything in sight. Jim was unable to make out the man's facial features, but he could see that this man was wearing a gray tailored three-piece suit. He wore a white-gold ring with a ruby center on his right pinky finger. The man's light blue eyes seemed to pierce through Jim as if with a samurai blade.

Agonizing fear swelled throughout Jim's body; it was so terrible, that he arose in his bed. Jim felt like he was having a panic attack— he was sweat profusely and unable to breathe. As the horrifying dream finally ended, he had a flashback of his past. Jim went back to six years in the past, before all the events unfolded and when it all began.

2

Jim lay on the bed in the fetal position with his eyes closed. *Dreams—oh, how they haunt me!* he thought. *I always have a way of remembering dreams. That friggin' guy or shadow keeps popping up in a lot of my dreams. I wonder what it means. Who is that guy anyway? Why does he constantly appear in many of my dreams and always have an eerie, malevolent laugh? I thought that he would just disappear, but he refused, like he wanted to torment me day and night.*

The laugh would wake Jim in a dreadful sweat and cause him to pant for air. Many nights when he would wake, Jim would catch himself holding his breath. *If I keep holding my breath like that, then I guess I'll just die.* Jim thought, *Maybe he will one day actually succeed in killing me.* He rubbed the sleep from both eyes, as well as the tears that remained.

He rolled onto his back and placed his hands behind his head, interlocking his fingers. He yawned deeply and stared at the ceiling. It was always bothersome for him to get out of bed. While trying to fully wake up, Jim pondered aloud, "Why in the world do I stay up late but then hate waking up early and then do it all over again? I fight going to sleep, and when I finally do get to sleep, I hate waking up. I would sleep for a week if I could." He lay in bed, hating life, wishing it would just end. Ten minutes elapsed, and he still fought getting out of bed.

"The world is too perfect in the mornings. I simply don't have to worry about bills or about anyone for that matter."

He kept evaluating the pros and cons of getting out of bed and then he realized that thirty-five minutes had elapsed. He finally rose from his bed with the fullest bladder, which caused him to rush to the bathroom. He began to run through his day. "I know that today, just as every day, is going to be quite terrible and continue to give me almost no reason to live. I wish I had a job, and honestly, I just wish that I could wake up as a different person one day. My life has sucked from the get-go. Life just forgot about me and dealt me a crappy hand. If ever life was a person and I met him, I would drop-kick him across his face."

The phone rang, but Jim figured that it was a bill collector.

"All those people ever do is try to get the little money that I have. Oh, how I hate them!" The phone rang once more, and he contemplated answering. He racked his brain and figured that if this was a bill collector, he would talk in a funny accent that was barely understandable and have a laugh or two at the guy. Once again the phone rang, and with a chuckle, he picked up the phone and heard a woman on the other end.

"Hello," she said in a soft tone.

"Herroh," he said in a funny accent, doing all that he could to withhold bursting into laughter.

"I'm Jan from Simple Buy Grocery, and I'm calling for Mr. Ackelson."

Jim quickly corrected his tone of voice as he realized his mistake. He didn't want to make a fool of himself. His face felt hot and turned red from embarrassment. "Yes, ma'am, this is Jim Ackelson."

"Mr. Ackelson, I am calling you to notify you that your application for the assistant manager position here has been reviewed. Another individual who applied has changed his mind about the position, and now we'd like to fill his slot. We would like you to come in for an appointment today, in about an hour."

Jim was amazed and shocked; something good finally had happened to him. "That's awesome! I will definitely be there. You can count on me."

"That's good, Mr. Ackelson. I will be sure to tell Mr. Wright that you accepted the appointment. Have a nice day."

"You too, Jan," Jim said, and then he placed the receiver down. Jim quickly got dressed and fixed his hair, all while singing aloud and dancing. He walked to the front door with his résumé in one hand and his car keys in the other. His wallet was firmly placed in his back right pocket.

He stepped outside and saw a normal day as any. It was midday, and the sun beat down and scorched the asphalt. The sky was filled with carefree birds, caressing the sky with their wings, gliding ever so gently. The humidity was less than it had been yesterday, but the wind might have had a part to play with that; summer had just begun.

Jim was five foot eight and had smooth jet-black hair that he would occasionally slick back. Today, Jim wore a mediocre, light-gray pin-striped suit with white buttons. Jim locked the front door. He was excited that he'd finally landed a job interview as an assistant manager with the local grocery store. He was sporting a button-up shirt and a silver silk tie. If anyone were to see Jim, they would believe that he was either a businessman or a lawyer—until they saw his car. Jim slowly walked to his 2003 Ford Taurus with a tremor of nervousness. He opened the car door with a slight jerk, got in, and quickly fastened his seat belt.

Jim placed his key into the ignition and turned the key. The car made various grinding noises and sounded like it was starving for gas. He slammed on his horn and briefly hit the steering wheel and dashboard. "Why, God, why, on all the most important days, do you allow this to happen to me? Have you not done enough wrong in my life? Why is it that the universe despises me?" In his frustration, Jim forcefully pressed the seatbelt release button. The Seatbelt released and he kicked opened the driver's door. Jim kicked the door so hard that as he attempted to exit his vehicle, the door flung back and slammed into his head, causing a slight cut on his forehead. His face now was cherry red from anger and frustration. He was having a slight tantrum, kicking and thrashing the car door and the front fender. Finally, Jim opened the hood and murmured to himself, "Stupid car."

Jim was not particularly mechanically savvy, but he understood how to check the air in his tires and how to read the fluid levels. Jim grabbed a paper towel from the dashboard in his vehicle to check the fluid level of the oil. He was surprised that the oil level was quite low. He tried to remember the last time that he'd had the oil changed. After all, he had been busy, attempting to find a job. Jim thought, *Who actually has time to worry about a simple thing like that the oil? To top it all off, I got bills out the wazoo, $236.48 in my checking account, and all my bills are gonna hit in three weeks.* Jim inhaled deeply and held his breath for eight seconds before he slowly exhaled.

Regardless of his current predicament, Jim now only had fifteen minutes to get to his job interview. Jim took deep breaths so he would not take out his annoyance and frustration on his résumé. He now thought of all the hard work and all the classes that he'd taken in high school to prepare for the real world. That was seven years ago, but it only seemed like a leaf blowing in the wind, just seconds or minutes ago. "My, my, my, how the time has flown by. I cannot let this slow me down. Life is just full of let-downs," he said, while grinding his teeth together. He placed his resume on the hood of his Ford and slicked back his hair once more.

Jim now pondered how he would get to this interview. He thought of walking—it was summer, after all—but in his current clothes and in the summer heat, he believed that he surely would pass out or arrive looking less than professional. He knew that if he walked to the interview, he might barely make it on time.

Jim was the type of person who always was early. He had learned in his earlier years that being early was being on time, and being on time was being late. His lesson was reinforced when he was scheduled to attend a class field trip to an art museum. The trip was very important to him. He arrived late school and missed the field trip. He vowed that day to never again be late to anything.

Jim had decided that he wanted to arrive early so that he could practice scenarios and be better prepared. Against every desire that he had to not walk to the interview, something against his better judgment instructed him to do so. He could not quite put his finger on what directed him to walk, but he decided that whatever the reasoning, walking would be more beneficial. He believed that walking would build his confidence and alleviate the frustration that had built up.

Jim checked that his dress shoes were tied. He grabbed his résumé with a smile and walked down his driveway, thinking, *Well, at least it's only down the road, only just a couple of blocks. Besides, what else could possibly go wrong?* Jim was walking at a relatively quick pace; he wanted to keep his vow to always be early and never be late. He was now halfway to the grocery store, and everything seemed to be getting better. As he walked, he felt something pecking at his left foot. His shoelace had come undone and was jumping with every step. Jim hunched over to tie his shoe, but before he could finish, a homeless man with no teeth and a shopping cart full of random trash approached Jim.

The homeless man had an unpleasant smell, as if he hadn't bathed for weeks or months. He had mud caked to his forehead. His hair was long, matted together, and hung in dreadlocks. The soles of his shoes were separated so that they appeared to be talking, and the shoes had holes everywhere. The clothes that this man wore were as tattered as if he had served in battle.

His skin was oily, dirty, and covered with sunspots. "Excuse me, sir, may I please have a few moments of your time?" the homeless man said.

"Sorry, man, I just can't afford to spare any money or time," said Jim.

"But sir, it will only be but a few moments. Can't you show compassion to me? All I want is someone to talk to me," the homeless man pleaded.

"Man, you really don't get it. *I don't have time.* Just leave me alone. I'm busy and don't have time for you, for God, or for anyone for that matter," Jim barked.

"Sir, I have come to deliver an important message. One way or the other, you shall receive this message. You have been designated by the Most High to fulfill his will," said the homeless man with authority.

"Dude, you are whacked out your mind. I gotta go!" said Jim, walking away in almost a light jog to separate himself from this man. He started thinking of the trouble with his car and became angry again. Jim turned to yell at the homeless man, "Besides, there is *no* ..." The homeless man was now gone out of sight. "God."

Jim was quite disturbed by this image. The homeless man looked as though he had difficulties walking; how could he have run away? "That couldn't have happened. Maybe the guys are playing a joke on me again."

James Andros, Kyle Rodd, and George Sights had always been into playing practical jokes on everyone, especially since they were Jim's best friends. He had little time to dwell on this situation; the conversation with the homeless man had cost Jim five minutes, and he now had four minutes left on the clock until his interview. The summer heat was now at ninety-five degrees with 40 percent humidity. Jim began running, and sweat started to run down his face, neck, chest, back, and legs. The résumé whipped back and forth in the wind as he hauled down the road. Jim raced across the grocery store's parking lot, straight through the entrance door, and took a seat.

3

Jim was full of adrenaline and overly excited about his interview. He hoped that with his slick wardrobe and well-written résumé, he would be the best candidate for the position. He looked down at his watch and realized he was three minutes late. Jim's heart felt like it had dropped down a five-story building. "Mr. Ackelson, Mr. Wright, the manager, will now see you," said the assistant.

Jim's heart began to pound like a war drum, and his stomach filled with millions of fluttering butterflies.

Jim gave himself a good once over; he ran his hands through his hair and wiped the sweat from his brow. He knew he was as good as he would get and deemed himself appropriate to enter the interview. Jim cautiously viewed the room. In his opinion, this room was quite peculiar. It was painted a dark blue, with the American flag painted on the back wall behind Mr. Wright. There were pictures of Mr. Wright shaking hands with people who looked to be important. His desk had numerous pictures and a clock.

The clock seemed to be ticking into a microphone, but Jim realized that was only because his senses were enhanced from his nervousness. Jim's eyes finally landed on Mr. Wright. He looked to be in his mid- to late fifties. His hair was turning from gray to white. His face was wrinkled, but his eyes were a beautiful baby blue. Jim guessed that Mr. Wright weighed about two hundred pounds. He wore a white dress shirt with an American flag tie. He smiled at Jim, which Jim took as a good sign.

At least he is in a cheery mood, thought Jim.

"Hello, Mr. Ackelson. Please close the door behind you and have a seat," Mr. Wright said as he motioned to the chair in front of him. Jim quietly closed the door and shook Mr. Wright's hand, but he sat down with such a force that he almost missed the chair entirely. "Do you happen to have your résumé with you today?" questioned Mr. Wright.

Jim passed the creased résumé to Mr. Wright, who read it but looked concerned. "I see that you graduated high school, but you do not have any college experience listed," said Mr. Wright.

"Yes, sir, you are correct. I did not quite decide what I wanted to do with my life after high school. I had to start working after graduation, and since then, I haven't had the time or finances to attend college," explained Jim.

"I understand, Jim. Life can be challenging, and it demands much, but so does an assistant manager's job. What would occur if this position for which you are applying demands something that you cannot do? What will you do then? Will you just turn away and give up? We need a professional individual who can maintain a balanced life and work schedule. This individual must be capable of making decisions that ultimately may affect other employees. Can you honestly tell me that you are up to par and can play ball?" Mr. Wright spoke with an element of sternness in his voice.

Jim's heart felt as though it had been trampled upon by wild elephants, and he became more and more nervous—that was apparent by the visible amount of sweat running down Jim's forehead. His throat swelled as if he'd had an allergic reaction to bee stings, and he began a constant process of clearing his throat. Jim tried to think of something witty to say, so that he would sound as intelligent as a college student, and he finally responded, "Sir, I believe that I can hold any position or responsibility that I am tasked with. Although I may have not attended college, I have been in the workforce and have past experience dealing specifically with customers. I believe that I am fully capable of making decisions, and that with my leadership, I can help make this place more efficient."

"Well, thank you for your time," Mr. Wright said. "These are all the questions that I have for you at this moment. We will give you a call in a couple of days to notify you of our decision." Mr. Wright grabbed Jim's hand with such a firmness that Jim forgot the guy was old.

Jim left the room and slowly made his way to the front entrance of the store, his head hanging low. He hoped that Mr. Wright believed him because he sure didn't believe himself.

Just as Jim was exiting the store, he remembered that his car was drained of oil. He made his way to the small automotive section in the miscellaneous aisle. He grabbed four quarts of 5W20 oil and went to the self-checkout to make his purchase. Jim left the store carrying two shopping bags that each contained two quarts of oil. He crossed the parking lot and tried not to think about the interview. It felt impossible; his mind seemed to magnify every detail that had occurred during the interview. "God, I'm such a screw-up. It's always about school. I'd bet anything the other guys who went in before me had loads more schooling than I do. What am I ever going to do? I need this job to pay my bills. I hate being in debt. I feel like I'm drowning in it every day."

He continued to walk with his head down. *Don't walk with your head down, or you will never know where you're going,* echoed a vague memory from his mother. Jim alleviated some of his tension with a sigh. As he raised his head, he saw a woman walking his way. *She's probably on her way to the store that I've just come from.* She wore bright yellow flip-flops, beige shorts, a light blue tank top, and sunglasses. She was slender and about five foot three, and as Jim walked closer to her, he thought a weird aura surrounded her. Jim got chills, as if he was receiving strange vibes from her. She passed Jim with a mischievous smirk on her face. Jim was a little confused because he did not know her, but he didn't think much about it. He was far too concerned with the interview and all his past failures to worry about the look from a strange woman.

He continued to walk to his house but kept getting the feeling that he was being followed. He went left, he went right, he made some twists and turns, but he couldn't shake the feeling he was being closely watched and followed. Jim kept glancing over his shoulders, but found no one following him. The feeling came more frequent, and it seemed like someone was skimming the back of his dress shoes. He felt something creeping behind him, something lurking in the shadow of the day. Jim's body was covered with goose bumps, and a slight chill covered him. It seemed as though every hair on his body stood straight up.

Jim picked up his pace in a desperate attempt to escape the nothingness following him. He burst into a dead sprint, but the faster he ran, the stronger the presence grew. Jim felt enveloped by an invisible blanket. He felt dirty, just downright unclean. The feeling seemed to tear at his skin, muscles, and bones in every direction. All Jim wanted to do was curl up in a ball and rock himself. His insides seemed freezing and caused him to be extremely nauseated.

Jim saw his refuge when he turned the corner and saw his house. As soon as he touched the front door, all the ugliness melted away. Jim was drenched with sweat; he went to the kitchen and filled a glass with ice and water. He gulped down two glasses of water and gasped for air as his body tried to recover from his only run of the year. He went to the living room and plopped down on the couch, where he wallowed in self-pity as he wrapped his arms around himself. "Nothing ever goes right in my life," he whined. "I have no family, no job, and no money. I don't even have a girlfriend. I barely have any friends, and now I'm back at this small house again."

He searched through his DVD collection and found a pornographic DVD. Jim could not resist the urge to watch it. He'd had an addiction to pornography since he was first introduced to it by his friends, back in their freshman year of high school. He had attempted several times to break this addiction, but the urge was too strong. Self-pity and selfishness only added fuel to the fire as a voice began to defend his urges. *"Come on, Jim, what's so bad with showing a little love and affection to yourself? Who else is going to do this? It is human nature, after all. Besides, you can quit next time if you like. Jim ... come on. What are you waiting for?"* Jim began to smile as he gave into this uncontrollable addiction and went to push play.

Just then, a loud pounding sounded from the front door. Jim paused the DVD player with an aggravated sigh and went to see who was at the door. He looked through the peephole, but saw no one there. Jim gritted his teeth and angrily opened his door. He stomped outside and yelled, *"Y'all better leave me alone. I'm not in the mood to mess around!"* He turned around and slammed the front door. Jim locked the door and returned to his recliner. He grabbed the remote and went to press play. The opening credits came on the television. As Jim was getting in the mood, a man suddenly appeared out of nowhere in front of Jim's television.

4

The man that appeared in front of the TV looked to be a six-foot African American. He wore blue jeans and a yellow polo shirt, as well as a brown belt and brown dress shoes. Jim asked furiously, "Where did you come from? How did you get in my house? *You better answer me before I call the cops!*"

Jim's television and DVD player shut off as the man spoke. "How can you enjoy being with something so disgusting? I have been assigned and ordered to you by God! You believe that a man spoke to you earlier. Looks can be deceiving, for he was not a man; he is like me, an angel. He was instructed to deliver a message, but you refused to receive or accept it. My orders are to explain your purpose and role within God's will."

Jim became infuriated and full of rage. He fired back with questions. "God? What do you mean, God? There is no God! You cannot possibly expect me to believe that you are going to magically appear out of nowhere. You honestly want me believe that you are an angel? I am a man of reason and science. There is no God. I was brought up in the Catholic tradition, and as an adolescent, God was never there. He didn't save my family and did nothing for me. That's why I left that hocus-pocus bull that they preach and turned to the big bang theory. It makes much more sense to me to come from an amoeba than being created out of nothing but dirt and air from this God that you speak of. I don't care who you claim you are and who you claim to represent, but *get out of my house right now!*" Jim screamed. His eyes were watering, and his face turned bright cherry red.

"How can you be so blinded by the lies that the fallen one has told you? How can you not accept that God loves you unconditionally? He sent Jesus to die for you and take your place of sin, rather than you taking the full burden of debt that you could not bear or even remotely come to pay. Regardless of what you believe, you have been called upon by the Most High, and I shall fulfill my orders," said the angel with a kind but authoritative voice.

"How can you still talk about God? You claim this Jesus died for my sin. You sound just like the church. Who are you to tell me what I am to believe?" Jim demanded. "The words you speak disgust me entirely. God never proved himself to me. All the church ever said was to have faith and that Jesus was going to return. That book that they all read says it. All it's good for is for brainwashing people into believing that crap so that they can steal the people's money. It's already bad enough with the economic crisis that we are in now, but then a bunch of people come to steal the little money that they have. Apart from what you said, having God love me unconditionally—whatever, man! That's a crock of crap. I have never in my life met anyone who loves anyone unconditionally, so how can this God you speak of love me unconditionally?"

"You have many questions, but I have been limited to the amount of answers to give," the angel answered. "Our time is short, and you have much to do. We must go now."

At that moment the angel took Jim and moved faster than anything in this world. Within seconds, they appeared in what seemed to be a most perfect place. It was the best looking, smelling, feeling, and refreshing place ever. There were no clouds in the sky, and the temperature was all too perfect. It seemed to Jim that he was either in the best dream ever or in paradise.

"I was instructed to bring you here to heaven," said the angel. "You are here to learn valuable things to fulfill the will of God.

Follow me." The angel was not angry or irritated; he spoke with love and authority.

The angel grabbed an interesting-looking fruit from a tree. The fruit looked like a mixture of an orange, apple, and kiwi, but its colors were blue and yellow with silver dots. The fruit had such a pleasant scent—rich in lavender, vanilla, and strawberry. "In order for you to withstand the presence of God, you must eat the fullness of this fruit," the angel instructed. "It will strengthen you and will prevent your current state of being from being crushed by the almighty God. Praise be to God!"

Jim took an uncertain nibble of the fruit. The greatest rush of flavors passed through Jim's body. The fruit seemed to contain a taste of honey, milk, and every fruit that Jim ever had known or tasted. A ray of strength flowed through Jim's body that caused Jim to laugh with joy. Jim almost swallowed the entire fruit without chewing. Strength surged and pulsated throughout his every cell, tissue, muscle, and entity. He felt like he had the strength of Hercules. Jim began to laugh almost uncontrollably with the joy that he had. This was joy that he could not explain; it was also joy that he had never experienced in his life.

"We must go forth," the angel said. "The designated time has come. Let us go, so that you may see what God has ordained for you to see. This is no trick or joke. Believe and receive it."

Speed now seemed to be second nature; they achieved a great amount of distance in seconds. Jim arrived in front of a magnificent angel—an archangel. The archangel was glowing with an immense light. The angel wore a breastplate that was eloquently engraved and was made of what looked like platinum, silver, gold, and many gems. The archangel had long hair that looked as smooth as silk and as light as a feather. The archangel had magnificent wings that not even an eagle could rival. They looked to be made of silk, and one wing was at least twenty feet in diameter and ten feet in length. Jim guessed that the archangel was at least thirteen feet nine inches tall and well proportioned. Jim could not help but stare; he just wanted to gawk at this archangel. The archangel seemed to not pay attention to Jim or the angel escorting Jim. The archangel turned 180 degrees and flew into the distance.

"Who was that magnificent angel, and how come he has wings but you don't?" asked Jim.

"That was an archangel; he is one of the few to whom God has given wings. Archangels have extreme power and have been charged with great responsibility. The archangel that you just saw was Lucifer himself."

"Wait a minute—this doesn't make sense. How can Lucifer still be an angel and in heaven?" Jim asked. "Didn't he challenge your God or something and get kicked out? That is what little I remember from hearing in that church."

"I have been instructed to bring you here in this time," the angel explained. "This time is prior to the great battle between God and Lucifer. This is also prior to the creation and fall of mankind. This is part of God's will—for you to witness and understand what happened, so that what God has willed for you to do may come to pass. *Glory be to God!*"

"So let me get this right. God really has chosen *me* to do something important? He has instructed you to bring me here prior to the creation of man, which means that this is the beginning of the creation of time? And that was Lucifer that I just saw?"

"Yes, all of your questions are correct. Do not be alarmed by what is now about to occur," said the angel.

The heavens began to rumble and shake with great force. There was no comparison to the greatness of the force that was occurring. A great and powerful voice spoke. "Let us make man in our image. Let them have dominion over the fish of the sea, over the birds in the air, and over the cattle, over all the earth, and over everything that creeps on the earth,"* said God.

While God was speaking, Jim noticed that next to God stood two beings that emitted great rays of light. They were praising God, saying, "Glory to the Maker and Creator of life. Blessed is God.

Glory and praise be to God!" God then gathered dirt from the ground and breathed into it. Creation had just occurred in front of Jim.

Jim was amazed as the dirt immediately started to take form. Adam was created and was perfect in every way. Jim's mouth dropped open, and he fell to his knees, praising God in his greatness.

"Come, we must go forward in time," said the angel. The angel took Jim forward at a rapid speed into the Garden of Eden. "You are not permitted to eat of anything. You are here to learn what occurs," said the angel.

Jim and the angel appeared once more near Lucifer. Lucifer seemed to be acting suspiciously, just like an individual who has difficulty deciding whether to do the right thing. Lucifer continued to move back and forth, and as he did, his wings flapped beautifully and caused great winds to be formed. The majority of animals that were present drifted away from Lucifer, save for a serpent. The serpent was twelve feet in length and two feet in diameter, with arms that caused it to look like a giant caterpillar.

Lucifer spoke to the serpent. "Oh, great creation from God, may I go into your being and speak a word to the man that God has also created. God has ordained and called this other creation to be higher than you. He favors and loves man much greater than every other creation. May we go and speak to the woman that she may cause herself and Adam to eat of the forbidden fruit? If we do this then God will love us more once again?."

"I believe you, oh great Lucifer, for God has surely given you great authority and responsibility," said the serpent. "You speak the truth. You may come unto me that we may go and speak to the woman, that God may once again love us greater."

Lucifer entered the serpent and went to the woman and tempted her with the suggestion of eating of the forbidden fruit. Jim followed and watched in awe, thinking, *Is this really happening?*

The angel knew Jim's thoughts and said, "Yes, this is really happening."

Jim wanted to scream at Eve for eating the forbidden fruit. He had tears running down his cheeks and begged Adam not to eat of the forbidden fruit. Jim continued to watch as Adam and Eve received knowledge. Jim then heard the voice of God, and he began to tremble from the awesome power of it.

"Because you have done this, you are cursed more than all the cattle and more than every beast of the field; on your belly you shall go, and you shall eat dust all the days of your life. And I will put enmity between you and the woman, and between your seed and her seed; he shall bruise your head, and you shall bruise his heel."*

While God passed judgment on the serpent, the arms and legs vanished, and immediately, the serpent lay on its belly. The serpent was trying with great might to move but found it quite difficult to maneuver using only the muscles in its belly. Jim was saddened by what was to occur. He remembered from church the story of the fall of man and the judgment that was passed.

Then God turned to Eve and spoke with such authority. He passed the judgment that kicked Adam and Eve out of the Garden of Eden.

* Genesis 3:14–15

5

J im watched as God walked away with the two other holy beings. He gathered that these other individuals must have been Jesus and the Holy Spirit, due to the fact that God kept consulting with them.

"I have been instructed that we are to follow Lucifer," said the angel. "For the current time, that is your sole purpose."

"Hold on a second. I never saw anyone talk to you, so how were you instructed of anything? Another thing—I'm tired of just calling you 'angel.' What is your name? You do have a name, don't you?" asked Jim.

"I have been called Asrel by the Creator. I must reiterate the fact that I am an angel. I don't need anyone to talk in front of me for me to hear what is said. Mankind is childish in these manners for they cannot understand spiritual aspects. They confine themselves to the laws of their world and not the laws of God. To hear what God and the Holy Spirit are saying, you must first tune your ears. The closer you come to God, the better tuned your ears are to hear him," explained Asrel.

Asrel and Jim followed Lucifer to a field full of luscious grass and vivid flowers. The air flowed with a pleasant smell as well as pink and blue butterflies. The field was scattered with hundreds of angels who were singing praises to God. "Praise to God!" said Lucifer.

"Praise be to God!" recited all the angels.

"There has been a great falling of the creation of mankind. How can one of God's creation be disobedient and yet God spares his life?" Lucifer asked. "I call forth that God is not the God that we serve. The God we serve would not have allowed for such an atrocity to occur. How dare he make us under the foot of mankind, a creation that has free will? They have the ability to choose what they want and how they care to receive it. God never gave us the chance or gave such love to us. Follow me, that we may bring back the righteousness of our authority. I will guide you and be your god, for God made me full of authority to uphold the law. I will remove the God who did not give us a chance of free will, and I will love you more than any creation!"

The angels thought there was some truth in what this archangel Lucifer had just said. They knew that he had been charged over them as a leader. They began to perk up and cried out loudly, as if they were ready to run forth with strength and might for the first battle. Some took up their shields and swords. In the midst of what could be viewed as a riot or a mob, some angels rebuked Lucifer. "Father, may you grant us the strength to overcome and defeat this atrocity."

Another archangel came forth, charged by God to fight this battle. His wingspan was about half the size of Lucifer's, but the light that his body emitted was just as bright as Lucifer's. He did not have long hair; it was well groomed and a light brownish color. His face was full of seriousness and strength. His movements were smooth and swift, like a flowing, gentle river. His breastplate was platinum and had words inscribed in the center. His skin was fair and quite smooth, like milk and honey. Along with his armor he wore a scarlet robe that wrapped around his left shoulder. His shield looked lightweight and was polished to a fine finish; this was possibly the best type of mirror Jim had ever seen.

The archangel had a slender sword in his right hand. Even from a distance, Jim perceived that each side was perfect. Jim asked curiously, "Asrel, what is inscribed on that archangel's breastplate?"

"It says *Eeks Achweejal Miyendo Khaleadeel*, which means 'For the Glory of God,'" explained Asrel.

The archangel said with fury, "Lucifer, you foul beast, ungrateful and unholy. How dare you compare yourself to the God of all creation? I say to you that this very day you *shall* be stripped of the righteousness that encompasses you. You shall fall from the heavens this day and toil unto the end of time. You have a done a great evil unto God, and your judgment shall be greater than all!"

Speaking in a calm, cool, and collected manner, Lucifer responded, "Michael, how could you be so blind that you would believe the lies that God—your God—has said? We have all been lied to, but I know the truth. We were created by that false God and charged to withhold the law, which is the same law that *he* created. Join me, Michael, that we may overcome this false God. I know that this very day I shall overcome this false God, who is self-centered and does not uphold the law that he himself created. I was there to witness the fall of his beloved mankind. God told the man and woman to not eat of the forbidden fruit. When they ate the forbidden fruit, all God did was shun them from the garden. God then placed them on the earth and cursed it. He should have destroyed them! How can this God—this false God—dare say that he loves them more than he loves us? Michael, I shall not ask you once more, for if you are against me—the true god—I shall destroy you and your false God!"

"Lucifer, I have nothing more to say against you. I shall be there as the true God strips you and casts you out of the heavens," Michael boldly stated.

The heavens began to rumble and shake unlike anything witnessed. It seemed as though the heavens were trying to rip apart. Jim knew that this was due to the division in heaven. There seemed to be no peace, in Jim's view. Everything seemed to be in disarray. Michael and a few other angels began to fight with such fearsomeness. Jim saw what seemed to be a million angels arrive and join Michael. Jim also noticed that there were a few more archangels present in this epic battle. Bright sparks of lights were emitted as the angels clashed.

The army of God outnumbered those who had joined Lucifer. The archangels all made their way toward Lucifer. With each swing of their swords, twenty-two angels were catapulted in every direction. The archangels came at Lucifer from every direction. They were confident in their actions as they charged him. As the archangels clashed into Lucifer it sounded like fifteen hydrogen bombs had exploded at same location and time. A blinding light filled the air, as well as cries from the angels that were led astray. Lucifer was pinned down by the archangels; each had a limb or a wing.

"Bow before the Most High!" called a deep voice. All angels, apart from the archangels, bowed. Jim was throttled to the floor and lay prostrate; he could only glimpse at what was happening.

"Eat this, it will give you strength," said Asrel. "God has ordained that you are to watch what is happening and for you to learn. You are unable to withstand the glory of God. It overcomes you and causes you to lie on the floor."

Jim could only nibble at the fruit. He could not move any of the muscles in his body, apart from his eyes, eyelids, and his mouth. With each nibble and swallow of the fruit, Jim began to regain his strength. He watched as God approached Lucifer. Jim could hear cries of the misguided angels; he knew that they understood that they had accepted the greatest lie ever told. God stood next to Lucifer, who kept squirming like a fish out of water in attempt to free himself.

"Lucifer, you foul beast. I created you and glorified you above the rest," God said. "You have lied to and caused my beloved Adam and Eve to sin. You also lied to a third of my beloved angels. I love all my creation. Why could you not understand that? You have caused a division here in my heavens. I cannot allow you or the angels that followed you to remain in heaven. You claimed to be a god and accused me of being a false God. *I am the only and true God!* When I cast you down, I say to you that there shall be a day of reconciliation, a day of judgment. I shall send my beloved Son to defeat you. He shall claim authority over you and your followers. You want to be a god so badly, so I shall make you one. You shall, this day, be god of all that is not of good, the father of lies and the prince of the air."

The heavens shook with each word that God spoke. Lightning spread like a freshly woven spider web throughout the heavens. "I receive the authority, glory, beauty, and light in which I bestowed upon you and your followers. You are cursed this moment and down to the cursed earth shall you remain until the end times, until I come to pass the final judgment," said God.

Lucifer was the first to be stripped of everything. First was the light that emitted from his body. His body then began to deform into a hideous figure. His head began to tangle and twist, his eyes blackened, and his face lost its frame. It became concave and mangled. Bone punctured his skin, and there were several lacerations. In the end, Lucifer looked to be a shriveled, decaying body.

Jim thought, *He is the most disgusting figure that I have* ever *seen. And to think, this is what we have been scared of this entire time.*

As Lucifer's body began to transform, he could only scream in dire agony. The rest of the angels who had followed Lucifer began their transformation.

"Out into the cursed earth I cast you, you cursed and fallen beings," said God. God finished speaking and a rift in the barrier between heaven and earth opened up. The misguided angels had been cast out of heaven.

Lucifer made one last comment as he was cast to earth. "I swear by all that it is within me that I shall return and remove you from your throne. I shall destroy your creation, and they shall never return to you. I shall make them so wicked and perverse that all you can do is destroy them yourself."

J im seemed to be full of discontent and had a sense of uneasiness. Asrel urged Jim to get up and follow him.

"So that is why we endure so much crap back on earth?" Jim asked. "I thought that God said he loved us. Why then did he bring the flood and try to kill all of mankind?"

"You still rely on the knowledge of mankind. When will you learn to just trust in God? He did, after all, create you, and you are still alive. I constantly hear mankind begging for a miracle, yet when God provides a miracle, all mankind does is spit it back in God's face. Come, you have a destination with the Most High."

Jim knew that if he was in his earthly body, his hands would be cold and clammy. He knew his entire body would be drenched in sweat.

Asrel and Jim continued on their path along a golden brick walkway. All Jim could think was, *If only I could take one or two of these bricks back home, I would be out of debt and could get a new car.* They came to what Jim could best describe as castles, but these castles had no comparison to any building he had ever seen, heard of, or even dreamed of. They were laid with gold bricks that were each ten feet by ten feet. The castles were at least six hundred feet high and one thousand feet in length. The windows were made of a transparent material that was unlike any plastic or glass. It was almost as if he could stick his hand right through them.

The front door was magnificent and was a combination of cherry wood, red oak, and mahogany. There were also columns that favored the ivory pillars on plantation homes. Jim had to constantly withhold his jaw from dropping and his tongue from hanging out and drooling everywhere. He just kept looking up in attempt to find the roof of this castle. A memory surfaced from when he was a young boy. He remembered going downtown to a stadium and staring at the skyscrapers. The emotion left Jim in awe.

"I know what you are thinking," said Asrel. "Jesus spoke of these back on his earthly days. These are the mansions that our Father has built for his children. We do not have the luxury of time for you to explore these mansions, for your appointment with the Father is approaching."

As if Jim's legs had been attached to a mule, they moved on command from Asrel. Although they had an appointment with the Father, it seemed as though they were in no rush. Jim could not remember a more peaceful time; he felt carefree and relaxed. They had walked no more than five minutes when they arrived at a magnificent building. The mansions that Jim had just viewed had no comparison to this building.

The building never seemed to stop going up and resembled a coliseum. There was much noise as they neared the entrance of the building. As they entered the building, the entire coliseum-like building erupted with one unified voice. "Praise to God! Praise to God! Praise to God!" The further Jim moved inside this building, the more strength he lost. Walking was too difficult, so Jim tried crawling. Crawling then became difficult as well, so Jim tried to army crawl. Soon, he had no strength to move. Jim could only lie on the ground.

Asrel gave Jim additional fruit to consume. Once again, with each swallow of this fruit, he regained a little of his strength. As he crawled, he noticed the difficulty of moving. Even after eating the fruit, he showed no improvement. Jim's head felt like it weighed fifty pounds.

Jim halted at the base and center of a platform. The platform was about 120 feet in diameter and was covered with transparent gold. He caught a glimpse of the foot of the throne at the other end of the platform. He tried with all his might to look up at the throne but was once more throttled to the floor.

The only thing Jim could see was the color of pure and translucent white. There was no other way to describe the purity and strength that this throne emitted. One word to describe the color that Jim saw was glory.

Asrel beckoned him. "Behold, Jim, you are in presence of the Father."

The aura of God was so powerful that no matter the amount of the fruit that Jim consumed, he still could not do anything but lie prostrate and face the ground. Tears flooded from Jim's eyes. Jim could not remember the last time that he had cried like this. A deep sense of unworthiness screamed inside of Jim's head. "I am unworthy to receive your words, unworthy to be in or near your presence. Just kill me, God. I cannot bear the guilt that is upon me." Each word became more mumbled and caused him to stutter.

Tears continued to flow from his eyes, and his nose began to run with snot. The snot slowly trickled down and dripped onto the floor.

"My beloved son, why would you ask me to kill you, the creation that I love so much? You have been given the opportunity for the redemption of your sins through Jesus Christ. He was sent as the final sacrificial Lamb to die for your sins. All you have to do is believe in your heart and confess with your mouth that he died on cross for your sins and rose again three days later. If you accept this truth, then your sins will be paid in full and forgotten.

Salvation is a free gift. It is something that mankind cannot earn by his own effort. Mankind has fallen to darkness and sin; thus, he is separated from me. He has been away from me for so long that he cannot hear me. I send many messengers to spread the Word, my Word, but few will accept this. I have your task before you this day. You have witnessed the fall of Lucifer and a third of the fallen angels.

There are numerous evil things that search the earth for peace. They cannot ever accomplish this. So they do all they can to dwell in my temples. Lucifer has continued to uphold his vows by causing them to blanket themselves with sin; thus, guilt is followed. He does all that he can to make me pass judgment, but only through Jesus do I refrain. Indeed, a day of reconciliation is approaching, for my Word never returns void to me."

God finished with, "When you finally accept Jesus as your Lord and Savior, I shall envelope you with an anointing. You are to go into the third-world countries and the countries that reject my only begotten Son. In those places, you shall face many obstacles and trials. You shall face demons, giants, corrupt animals and beasts of the land, and Satan himself. Worry not, for my anointing and the Holy Spirit will guide you. I shall charge my angels to watch over you. From here, you shall walk a little more to hear from my Son. Go forth." The words that God spoke were full of authority; they were stern, yet so full of love, peace, and compassion. Jim became especially full of the peace that God had administered to him.

Jim slowly turned and crawled away from the presence of God to the feet of Asrel. Asrel bent over with a smile and gave Jim more of the divine fruit to eat. Once Jim had received enough strength to rise to his feet, Asrel pulled him up almost instantly. Jim continued to eat the fruit until a joyous emotion climaxed. Jim jumped up and screeched, "*Praise be to God!*" In unison, a choir echoed and sang, "Praise be to God! Praise to the God of glory, the God of mercy, the loving and the Almighty, Alpha and Omega! Hosanna, Hosanna, Hosanna!"

Jim and Asrel laughed hysterically all the way out the entrance. They arrived once more on the walkway of gold but continued to walk into a field. The field was full of trees of all shapes and sizes. Even the trees worshipped God with songs of praise.

Asrel led Jim to a gently flowing stream. The water was so crystal clear that it looked like diamonds. The stream looked refreshing. Jim couldn't resist the urge to drink from it and rinse his face off. "Asrel, just wait a moment, please. I wish to refresh myself." Jim began to drink from the stream. The liquid brought an enormous rush of energy, almost like the divine fruit, yet it was smoother than water. The fluid tasted like manna and smelled delightful. Jim splashed water in his face and could only smile with comfort. While splashing the water in his face, Jim noticed a pair of feet walking toward him. Jim thought, *That's funny; I don't hear anyone walking or splashing water, for that matter.*

Jim was not startled when the feet stopped in front of him. Jim looked up and almost immediately fell to his knees. He cried out, "I'm so sorry. I'm not worthy. Forgive me." The figure standing in front of Jim was about five foot seven. His hair was a luscious light brown, and he had a face full of love. He wore the whitest robe and a crown. It was Jesus.

"Why do you not accept the gift that I have given? You refuse to accept because you believe that you cannot possibly do anything to receive this gift. I tell you the truth that no amount of works that you do on earth can get you back here to heaven and in the grace of God. All you have to do is believe in your heart and confess the truth. You do know that there were over five hundred witnesses there that day who saw me die and be resurrected? I am the Way, the truth, and the life. It is only by decree of the Father that you were able to be in his presence, but others will not have that opportunity. The next opportunity that they will have is on judgment day, when I come to pass the judgment. That day will be full of sorrow as well as rejoicing. I am here, speaking in front of you. All I have ever done is show love. Love is what I shall continue to show until the final day of judgment."

Jim was on the brink of an emotional breakdown and continued to sob.

"Cast your cares to me, and peace be unto you, Jim."

Immediately, Jim had a significant amount of peace flowing throughout his body, allowing him to speak. "Jesus, will you please forgive me, for I have been a sinner all my life, neglecting and rejecting you. I know that you are the only way for me to receive my redemption. I believe that you died that day on the cross and rose again on the third day. I know that you claimed victory over Satan. I accept you as my Lord and Savior of my life."

"Rise to your feet," said Jesus. Jim rose immediately and was welcomed with a big hug from Jesus. Jesus spoke into Jim's ear, saying, "That's all I ever wanted, for mankind to acknowledge the truth. I say to you that from this moment forward, your name is written in my Book of Life. It has been appointed that your time here has come to a conclusion, until you are called once more. You are to return home and rejoice with your family. Remember that I shall always reside with you and that I love you," said Jesus.

7

Jim blinked vividly, attempting to come out of this daze that he believed he was in. He looked down and could see his hands, his human hands. He looked around and saw the natural nothingness that always surrounded him. He began coming back into consciousness, and his thoughts started slowly picking up speed. Jim was now fully coherent and of sound mind. He argued with himself as to whether he had been asleep or daydreaming.

A man of science, he thought. *What would the guys think if I told them about something like this? No, no, no, I have been set in my ways, and this Jesus thing ain't for me. I must have run too friggin' hard on my way home.* Just as he was trying to put the notion of the Father, the Son, and the Holy Spirit to rest and away from him, he heard a deep voice call out from behind him.

"The Father has declared that you go into the world. You must leave," said Asrel. Jim nearly jumped out of his chair when he heard Asrel, the angel. He turned to see Asrel standing in front of him, as clear as day. Jim rose briefly, but in doing so, his legs buckled underneath him. His brain took longer than usual to process this command. "Your visit to heaven has drained you of your physical strength," Asrel explained. "You must feed your flesh as well as your spirit."

Asrel assisted Jim to his feet and gave Jim a glass of water from a nearby table. "I must leave you at this moment. You are to continue on your own for a short time," stated Asrel.

Jim began to panic. "Wait—you cannot leave me. I am new to this whole thing. I don't know what to do, you just can't leave me. I never thought this was real. I believed that there was no God or Devil, much less a heaven or hell. So what am I to do if something arises, like I run into a bad guy or a demon? I really don't think God will come down and defend me."

Asrel listened to Jim plead his case, but his stare was expressionless. Asrel exited the room in the same manner that he had entered it.

Jim was confused and full of questions, most of which contained "why me?" He felt alone and dumbstruck. He had no clue what to do or where to start. As he contemplated his next actions, he scratched his head. As a testimony to what Asrel had said about hunger, Jim's stomach began to gurgle, like an old, rusty machine that was turning over. Jim slightly winced as he clutched his stomach and went to the kitchen. When Jim entered his kitchen, he noticed how different it looked now, compared to when he arrived in heaven. His senses seemed to be working in a different aspect.

The white wall looked a little brighter, and the countertops looked a bit more refined. The floor needed to be mopped, and the table needed the clutter removed. Jim's attention was soon adjusted as his stomach griped at him for food. He grabbed the handle on the fridge and yanked it open. Jim raised his eyebrows in disappointment. Regardless of opening the refrigerator numerous times and seeing the same few items, Jim always anticipated seeing a fridge stocked full of goodies.

Aggravated and frustrated, Jim thought, *Great. Just some spoiled milk and butter.* Jim closed the fridge and began to rummage through his pantry. To his astonishment, he found two packs of roast chicken-flavored Ramen. A slight grin appeared on Jim's face as he nodded his head slightly and said, "All right."

He went to the cabinet next to the fridge and removed a medium-sized ceramic bowl and a black pot. At the sink, he filled the pot about halfway with water. Jim then opened both packets of Ramen, dumped the noodles in the water, and placed the pot on the stove, turning the burner to the highest setting.

Jim then sat at his small kitchen table and stared at the walls, looking for an idea. As Jim glanced at the walls, he realized that he had only one picture of his family, taken before his family was broken and separated. His life, as he knew it, was plain but always was full of resentment, lack of fulfillment, and pain. He thought back to all the painful events that he'd had to endure and wondered why God would allow such travesties to occur in his life. The memories visually appeared in his mind instantaneously. He focused his attention toward one childhood memory in particular. This memory, he believed, was the marker in his life for all bad things to come. Everything in his life had been perfect until that moment.

Nostalgia overtook him as he returned to his youthful age of ten. His family was separated through divorce. Jim always felt unhappy about that situation. He knew that what happened was not his brother's or sister's fault. He just wished that everyone would be happy, but he knew otherwise. Jim had invited his best friend, Arthur, over for lunch and then they were going to head to the park on their bikes. Jim and Arthur loved going off by themselves, to ride throughout the entire neighborhood—this was Jim's only measure of escape. They constantly timed themselves to try to beat their previous record. Jim was fairly competitive, but his anger would overcompensate with a greater measure and Arthur would tell him that he was a sore loser.

Carlene, Jim's grandmother, made freshly squeezed lemonade, whipped mashed potatoes with country gravy, green beans, and hearty beef stew. Jim and Arthur nearly swallowed their food whole in an attempt to get on the road.

"Jim, you know better than that, sweetheart," his grandmother said. "You need to slow down and chew your food with your mouth closed. Either way, you are going to have to wait for your food to digest before you can ride your bike. Arthur, honey, that goes for you too."

"But !" exclaimed Jim.

"No buts, mister. Butts are for sitting, and that's exactly what you are going to do until your food digests."

Jim huffed and puffed with disappointment but finally came to an agreement with his grandmother. Jim and Arthur finished lunch and placed their dishes in the sink. They then headed to Jim's room to play. Along with riding their bikes, they loved playing with action figures and army men; after all, that was every kid's dream. They grabbed the army men and began strategically setting them up for the epic battle that was about to commence.

Time flew by, and an hour later, they realized that they could leave. Jim searched for his grandmother to ask her permission. He looked around the entire house but didn't find her; instead, he found his dad. Jim's dad seemed like a giant to Jim, but he stood only five foot eleven. He had broad shoulders, a scruffy face, a good tan, and thick hair and thick sideburns.

"Dad, I can't find anywhere. Is it all right if we go ride our bikes?"

"Sure, son, you can go but under one condition—you take your brother with you."

"But Dad, you don't understand. He's no fun, and this is not fair!"

"Jim, if you keep up that attitude with me, we're going to have a serious problem, and you definitely will not be allowed to go."

"Fine. He can come, I guess." Jim wanted so dearly to complain and do everything he could to prevent his brother from coming. Jim and his brother, Shaun, were a year and a half apart, and like most siblings, they always were bickering and fighting.

Shaun was six inches shorter than Jim. He had a head full of light brown hair that reminded anyone who saw him of the Beatles in their earlier years. His face was smooth, like butter. He had very light brown eyes, a button nose, and a hint of freckles. Jim always felt like his parents loved Shaun more, and he believed that they did more for him as well. Jim dragged his feet to his brother's room, although he wanted to stomp his feet the entire way.

"What do *you* want, dweeb?" asked Shaun.

"Gr-r-r … you gotta come with me and Arthur. You know that Dad won't let me ride if you don't come," explained Jim.

"Well, what are you going to give me in return? If you want me to come so bad, why don't you beg for it, hmm?" replied Shaun. "You know what? You're a friggin' jerk."

Jim immediately positioned his body for attack and threw a couple of punches at Shaun's chest and upper arms. Like most situations, Jim was caught red-handed assaulting his brother, who was crying aloud. This attracted their dad's attention.

Jeff grabbed both of the brothers by their necks and pulled them apart. He held on to their necks, as he knew that they would be back at it again once he did. "What's going on in here? Jim, what is the matter with you? What provoked you to hit your brother?"

Jim was flustered, and his face was red and angry. Jim did want to speak to his dad. He knew that if he spoke, the anger would overcome his mouth, and tears would fall down. Jim held his breath, gritted his teeth and forced the blood to his head. As he did, his veins popped out on his neck and forehead. Jim's dad noticed that Jim was flustered and that his face continued to darken with a deep redness; Jim was now turning purple in the face.

"Breathe, son, you must breathe." Jeff grabbed Jim and started slapping his back in attempt to jump-start his lungs to function properly. This was a little too late for Jim; he passed out from anger and no oxygen. Jeff continued to slap Jim, and Jim finally coughed and began to breathe. His dad picked up Jim and carried him to his bed. Jeff turned his attention toward Arthur, "Son, I think it would be best if you went home."

"Dad …"

"Not now, Shaun."

Jeff stepped out into the hallway and told Shaun to follow him to the kitchen. Shaun lowered his chin and dragged his feet, as if he were wearing shackles. Shaun finally managed to catch up to his dad and sat in an empty chair that was farthest from his dad.

"Shaun, let's go to the store and get some food. On the way home, we will stop and rent a movie."

"But aren't you gonna ask me what happened?"

"Son, there are times that you must wait so that you don't let your emotions overcome your judgment. Do you understand this?"

"Yes, sir. But aren't you mad at me? Aren't you mad at Jim? He started it, after all. I did nothing at all."

"Shaun, what did I just tell you? You just blatantly told me to my face that you understood what I said. Unless you want me to punish you for what happened, I suggest that you refrain from asking those questions. It's pretty cloudy outside and looks like a bad storm is coming. Now go and grab your coat it's starting to get dark outside. From what I hear from the weatherman that it's supposed to rain," said Jeff.

Without any further arguing, Shaun went to his room and grabbed his neon-orange fleece sweater. Jeff was waiting at the door with the keys and an umbrella. "Let's go! Hurry up, Shaun. I don't want to get home too late."

Several hours passed, and all the while, Jim continued to sleep. He awakened quite groggy and startled by the thunder outside. The house was devoid of light, and the only sound was from the rain and thunder. The phone rang from the living room and caused Jim to jump up out of his bed. He managed to find the light switch and turn it on. The phone continued to ring and ring. "All right already. Gosh."

He walked to the living room and saw his grandmother answer the phone. Her face was covered with sadness. He could hear her voice began to crack as he could hear her fighting the urge to cry. Carlene hung the phone up and turned to see Jim standing behind her.

"Oh, my goodness, I'm so thankful you weren't hurt."

"What are you talking about,?"

"Oh Jim, it's just so terrible. Your dad has been in an accident and he's in the hospital!"

"Wait—"

Several emotions swelled inside of Jim. He quickly returned to his room and put on his shoes and was ready to leave. He rushed back to the living room and saw his. She was wearing a rain jacket and was covering her hair with a newspaper. It was apparent that she'd left the car running, and her headlights beamed at the garage. No words were exchanged as they closed the front door and left the house. Jim got in the backseat, buckled his seat belt, closed the door, and stared out the window. His grandmother made several attempts to speak to Jim, but Jim remained silent. He was lost in his thoughts while fighting the urge to cry.

They finally arrived at the hospital. Carlene tried to motivate Jim to get a move on. Jim couldn't bear to know the outcome of the accident and dreaded every step that he took toward the door. The rain made matters worse. Jim thought of the funerals that his family had attended that were all on rainy days. They walked to the entrance, and the doors slid open. On the floor were water-hazard signs, and a janitor was mopping the excess water from the floor. The Janitor also was cleaning up the dirty footprints that were left on the tile floor.

The assistants at the desk were talking among themselves and laughing at the jokes they made; they seemed to be enjoying themselves. Jim stood far from them to isolate himself, while Carlene asked the whereabouts of Jim's dad. Jim heard Carlene gasp as she found out the location. She approached Jim. "Jim, they said your dad and Shaun are both in the intensive care unit. We need to get up on the third floor quickly." She grabbed Jim's arm and practically pulled him to the elevator. The elevator ride seemed like it would never end; it was slow and needed maintenance and a thorough cleaning. Finally, the elevator came to a halt, and the doors opened briskly. As they exited the elevator, they saw that the intensive care unit was on the right side.

Machines beeped and sounded like they were breathing. Carlene made her way to unit number three and entered the through the curtains. Jim did not know what to think or how to act. *This will be as it always is in my family*, he thought. *Never a good ending.* Jim stopped at the foot of the bed and slowly lifted his head to see his dad. His dad's face had a few bandages over his left eye and stitches across his right cheek. Carlene could only tell Jim to stand by Jeff's side.

Jeff was unconscious and had several IVs in both arms. Jim placed his hand on top Jeff's hand. Immediately, Jeff's eyes shot open, and they were full of fear. He sat upright, looked into Jim's eyes, and cried out, "Oh-h-h-h God, please no, please, please, please no! Jim, you must prepare ..." Jeff's heart rate went from eighty-five beats per minute to 130 beats per minute. With every pause, Jeff choked and gasped for air. The machines that were monitoring Jeff sounded an alarm. Jeff's eyes were wide open and bulging. His pupils were pinpoints. Jeff gritted his teeth and barely had enough strength to let out the last of his words, stating, "He knows who you are ... and ... your ... purpose."

Jeff's heart rate was at two hundred beats per minute, and then it flat lined. The nurses and doctors rushed in, and in the process knocked Jim to the floor. Time slowed down to the point where everything was a frame-by-frame movement. Jim's head slammed against the cold hard floor and bounced at least four inches. Jim's eyes slowly blinked as his surroundings began to fade until his eyes closed and his body lay motionless.

8

Jim awoke to an eerie silence—it was the uneasiness that caused Jim to open his eyes. He felt as if he was surrounded by darkness. To his surprise, there was still a little light from the moon that was shining just over the tall fir trees. He was curled up in the fetal position in the middle of a road. He did not understand where he was or how he could have possibly come to be at this place. There was a fog not too far from where he lay. Jim noticed the fog making its way toward him. Within two minutes, he knew that he would be entirely enveloped by this fog.

Jim rolled on to his stomach and pushed himself to his knees. Quickly mustering the strength, Jim stood up and found it was quite easy to move. He felt lightweight and full of air, yet he had the notion that shackles were attached to his ankles. The shackles wrapped around his legs multiple times but had fallen to the floor. The chains that were attached to these shackles stretched as far as he could see. Jim decided to see how far he could walk. "I sure don't want to get stuck in the middle of the road and have an oncoming vehicle smack into me." While moving his feet, he stated, "This is kinda weird, being able to walk. It's like these shackles are a hologram or something." It finally dawned on Jim. "Great—another friggin' dream. But where am I? What purpose does my brain have to serve me with this crap?"

Without an objective in mind, Jim decided to run away from the fog. The fog began to play on some deep, forgotten fear as it enveloped him. Jim felt like the fog injected fear into his veins. His heart pounded as it screamed with fear. This jump-started his legs, as he started moving forward. Immediately he trailed to the side of the road. Without a clue as to what lay ahead, he kept a steady pace. Jim figured that it was the best option he had, considering that he could only see the fog. The fog appeared to have absorbed the sky.

A saxophone sounded, and Jim felt compelled to find it. He felt it was whispering, saying, "Jim ... Jim ... come to me. I long for you." Jim thought, *I must be either hypnotized or crazy.* With each step he took, the whispering grew stronger, as did his urge to find this saxophone. As time elapsed, he began to hear other instruments. *This,* Jim thought, *is an advantage, considering the denseness of the fog.* The fog was so dense that he could not see anything in front of him.

Jim remembered watching horror movies and always found it difficult to fall asleep. On several occasions his dad would explain that the horror movies used different scared tactics. One scare tactic was the eerie music they played to grab the attention of the viewer; this was how they made their money. The memories of those days back flowed from Jim at that moment. He kept feeling something nicking at the back of his heels as he ran. Something was definitely trying to grab him—or at least he thought so.

The music was close now and so crystal clear, it was like a party in his ear. In the distance, the building lights cut through the fog and shone in his face. A deep instinct told Jim that he was not out of the clear; he was still surrounded by fog. With his remaining energy, Jim ran as fast as possible to escape the fog. The race finally ended. Jim nearly fell over as he came to a complete halt. He hunched over, heavily gasping for precious air; he felt as if his lungs were about to burst. Jim moved his eyes from the ground to an unexpected town. The buildings were rundown and were more like huts. The air turned from gloriously clean and crisp to seriously flat. The townspeople walked around, looking like they had not eaten in days. Each person had long hair that was matted together. Some had pieces of flowers or sticks in their hair.

Jim absorbed the moment and remained still, allowing the cool air to splash against his face. Sweat streamed from every pore, and every muscle ached, as did his brain. He still could not understand where he was or what was happening. He expected a technology-enriched area, but he found the type of people that he might find in *National Geographic*. The inhabitants did not seem to recognize Jim. It was either that they could not see him, or they had no reason to care about his presence. Jim had an unpleasant gut feeling that he was expected to be there.

The road was now a dark burgundy color. The area lacked green vegetation, but there were chickens and goats milling about. The music began again and, like a magnet, drew him toward it. Jim lost the ability to care for his safety; he just had a burning desire to find this music. As he walked past a group of people and caught a glimpse of several unknown faces. These people looked torn; their faces had numerous scars. They also had wrinkles around their eyes and all across their cheeks. They held a look of expectation, and they became impatient with each passing step. Jim closed his eyes and allowed the melody to serve as his guide.

The tune playing thumped just like a heartbeat and then transformed into drums slamming together, like the call for war. Jim stopped and finally came across a large and ordinary hut. He entered the hut, but he felt lost and misplaced. His eyes adjusted to the dark bitterness of the room. There was a makeshift stage at the back of the room and a long table where a few people sat. Some of these people were the inhabitants of this land; others were well dressed and looked as though they had just returned from a rather formal party.

The desire to find the saxophone and lovely melody had faded all together. Jim's body began barking orders at his brain, telling him to sit and get something to drink. He craved water with a hint of lemon. He asked the server for water. The server quickly brought a dark brown plastic glass, served with a lemon attached to the rim. The server rarely said more than two words. Jim had many questions to ask him, but he decided to quench his body's demand.

Jim assessed what had happened this day and slammed the glass down. The server quickly reached for the glass and provided a refill. The condensation began to accumulate on the outside of the glass. Jim grabbed a plain napkin and moved to wipe it. Prior to placing his hand against the glass, he noticed a man to his immediate right wearing a white suit and a matching cowboy hat. The man spoke a few words to the server and chuckled to himself.

This man brought a great uncertainty to Jim's mind. The man turned his head in Jim's direction and said, "My, my, it sure is a fine day, a fine day indeed, good sir. Say, young man, what is your name? I do reckon that I have never met you, nor have I ever seen you 'round this neck of the woods."

Jim waited a few moments before he replied. "Sir, to be honest, I don't know where I am," Jim answered. "I just remember waking up in the middle of the road, and I began running. Can you please tell me where I am? What is so important about this neck of the woods?"

"Well, Jim, I'm glad that you asked that. I should tell you that you should turn away from your journey. I assure you that you will not finish what is required of you." The man pulled a long machete from the side of his leg, raised it above his head with his right hand, and placed his left hand on Jim's shoulder. Jim's heart felt like it dropped to his feet, and his lungs temporarily stopped working. Sweat formed all over his body.

The man smiled with evil glee through his crooked teeth. Everyone else in the room saw what was happening, but they did not move an inch; they kept to themselves. Inhaling deeply, Jim replied, "I don't know who you are, mister, but I don't take any crap, and I'm not about to start taking it from you. I will do what I want, and there is nothing you can do to stop me."

The man said, "This is my neck of the woods, and you're gonna die."

Another set of footsteps came running from the entrance. The footsteps belonged to another man, who slammed against Jim and tackled him to the floor. Jim felt like he had been hit by a bus. He was pressed to the ground and out of breath. The man that hit Jim was a redhead with a thick mustache and light blue eyes.

Jim could have sworn that he was going mad and in a daze. The man with the machete had moved with intense speed behind the man who had tackled him. The guy with the machete raised it and went for the blow to kill either Jim or the guy who tackled him. As the man swung downward with the machete, time slowed down, and the man who tackled Jim spoke in a soft country accent, saying with a gleeful smile, "Jim, it's time for you to go. You do not have to worry about this situation, for he cannot do anything to you. I tell you assuredly that you must wake up."

9

Jim blinked vividly as his sense of smell brought him back to reality. As he returned to the present time, his stomach gurgled and moaned. The water had been boiling for almost an hour and had evaporated. The noodles sounded like they were frying from the heat of the kitchen stove. "Oh no, please, oh please, oh please. They simply cannot be burned—that's all I have to eat." Jim's eyes slowly began to water as his hunger pains forced his mind to react. Jim turned off the burner and moved the pot to the back burner to cool down. He was now in a predicament, with not a bite to eat. Jim decided to drink as much water as he could to mask his roaring stomach.

Jim grabbed the glass of water from the kitchen table—the same glass Jim had been drinking from in the living room. He stepped in front of the kitchen sink and opened the faucet full blast. He placed his glass under the streaming water and watched the glass fill to the brim. He turned off the faucet, and the stream came to a stop, with a few drops of water clinging to the faucet.

Jim brought the full glass to his lips and let the water flow down his throat. A couple of loose streams fell down Jim's cheeks and chin. He drank the water without pausing for a breath and began panting like a dog as he finished. Jim placed the glass next to the sink with a small thud and wiped his face with his forearm. It was quiet all around—an awkward silence. Jim placed his hands on either side of the sink and he leaned forward, dropping his head low. He stared at the bottom of the stainless-steel sink and watched the droplets of water slowly make their way toward the drain. His brain remained full of everything that he had experienced today—it was all too much. He felt caught up in his own little world, until his phone rang.

Jim placed the receiver to his ear with a great deal of suspicion. He said nothing, as he kept his safeguards in place in the event that it was an irritating bill collector.

"Hello, this is Jan from Simple Buy Grocery. I am calling to speak with Mr. Jim Ackelson. Is he available?"

Jim's safeguards dropped, and his heart began to ferociously pound. It took Jim several moments to clear his throat; his nerves nagged at him.

Jim thought, *Please, oh please, God, let this be the day. I need the money and can't bear these bills pilling up.*

"Hello? Hello? Is Mr. Ackelson available?"

"Mmm-hmm … Sorry about that, Jan. I was having difficulty clearing my throat."

"Hello, Mr. Ackelson. I am calling on behalf of Mr. Wright to inform you of his decision on the position of assistant manager."

Jim's heart was beating as fast as a race horse's. A smile began to form as his excitement intensified.

"Mr. Ackelson, I am sorry to inform you that you were not selected for the position of assistant manager. We do, however, want you to know that we value your patronage at Simple Buy Grocery. You are always welcome to shop for your daily needs. Have a good day, Mr. Ackelson." Jan sounded quite enthusiastic.

Jim felt betrayed and believed that Jan was sadistic. "How can that woman sound so perky and enthusiastic about delivering bad news to people? There definitely should be a law about that or something, where the person delivering bad news must also deliver five hundred dollars. Yeah, I bet that would show them a lesson, at least to their pocket books." Jim was flustered, hungry, and still confused.

"God …" Jim took a deep breath and sighed heavily. "God, I was in your presence today. I never would have guessed that all this was possible. For once in my miserable life, I actually felt completely satisfied and cared for. Then, all of the sudden, I am back here in my mundane life, hungry, and receive bad news. What does a guy have to do to get a break? You know that this really isn't fair. I know that I am talking to you, probably blabbing your ear off. How do I know that you are actually listening? I sure don't hear you responding. Well, are you gonna say something or wha—" Jim was cut short when the phone rang again.

The ringer sounded louder and more annoying. "What now?" he exclaimed. Jim grabbed the phone and yelled, "*What do you want?*"

"Jim, sweetie, why are you yelling, dearie? You are hurting my ears. Can you please lower your voice?"

Jim was caught by complete surprise when he realized that his grandmother was on the phone. "Oh … sorry 'bout that, . I just got some bad news, and bill collectors keep calling my house. I really am fed up with those bill collectors; I really just wanted to tell one of them off."

"Well, I really am sad to hear that you're not doing so well. The reason I called is because I made way too much food for myself. I want you to come over. After all, I have not heard from you in a while." His always had a way to soothe and calm Jim, even during the most stressful of times.

Jim still was confused until his stomach gurgled and growled. The sound was quite interesting; it sounded like stray cats trying to sing Christmas carols in an alley. "Grandma, I gotta throw some clothes on, and then I will be over in a jiffy. I hope you made enough to feed a horse, because I am *hungry* enough to eat like one."

Jim's grandmother chuckled over the phone. Without saying good-bye or "see you later," Jim slammed down the receiver and ran to his room. He ran a little too fast and banged against the walls and the sides of the furniture. Jim's stomach still was barking orders at him to move faster and eat anything. Jim rushed to his closet and put on the first T-shirt and pair of blue jeans that he could find. Jim then grabbed a pair of white ankle high socks from his dresser drawer.

Jim dashed for the front door, and as soon he touched the doorknob, his brain took over his actions. "Keys … motor oil—oh great, I forgot." Jim headed to his garage and began to rummage through shelves for a funnel. The hunger pangs motivated him to move faster than usual. As happens when in a hurry, Jim knocked down books, articles, and old photographs from the shelves. One picture caught Jim's attention and caused him to stop in his tracks—it was of his brother, Shaun, and his dad, mom, and him. The picture frame had dust on the now broken glass.

Jim wiped the dust off the broken frame and reminisced about the few happy moments that he had as a complete family. Still confused about what had happened with his family, Jim tilted his head and noticed the oil-stained funnel covered by a red shop rag. Jim grabbed both the rag and funnel and headed back inside.

Jim grabbed the plastic grocery bag with the quarts of motor oil, and with keys in hand, he headed to his Ford Taurus. Jim placed the motor oil, funnel, and rag on the ground and then opened car door to pull the hood handle. The hood made a slight *thump* sound. The sound startled him, and Jim stood up in a hurry, hitting his head against the roof of his car.

Biting his tongue, Jim mumbled under his breath, "Friggin, stupid, dumb car." He slammed the door shut and then went to the hood. It took him a frustrating five minutes to find the latch under the hood, and Jim continued to mumble under his breath in anger.

He propped the hood open with the metal rod and narrowed his eyes as he grabbed the engine oil reservoir cap. After removing the cap, he grabbed the rag, two quarts of oil, and the funnel and poured the oil into the reservoir. This ordeal was taking longer than he expected and anger began to build like a small forest fire. Gritting his teeth, he had the strongest urge to start complaining about everything.

"I just don't understand—this is all too real. Why is my car the way it is, and how do I let myself get into these situations? Why? Why? Why? Why?" A small breeze whipped toward Jim, and as it hit him, a soft, gentle, and nourishing voice spoke in an amplified whisper. The voice was strong inside his body, saying, "Be at peace." Not knowing what to say, Jim instantly shut his mouth and finished his task.

Jim closed the hood and started his engine. He was fascinated by what had just occurred. He had strength from the overwhelming peace and love that filled his body. Excited, Jim backed out of his driveway and made his way toward his grandmother's. He had been driving for only ten minutes when another strange sensation came over his body—but the sensation was not a pleasant one; it was cold and empty, similar to the one he'd experienced earlier that day. His body began to sweat, and a searing headache formed.

His body became numb, and his mouth dried up. White spots formed on his tongue. His vision went in and out of focus until everything became hazy. His nose began to burn as if he'd just caught a whiff of pepper spray until it finally clogged. His muscles convulsed in his arms, legs, and abdomen. Jim knew he had to get to his grandmother's, if only so he would not crash and injure someone along the way.

Jim was in agony, and his only hope was to cry out. He tried to cry out the one name that would save him. Every attempt he made to speak was followed by agonizing pain. It felt as though someone was strangling his neck. After that, it felt like someone was piercing his tongue and cheek with a scalding metal skewer. The pain was so immense that he had to pull over to the side of the road. His eyes watered, and his breathing was restricted to a rapid and shallow breath.

With a final attempt, he spoke aloud. "Jesus." Instantly, a giant weight lifted from his body. The hold on his neck loosened, and his breathing returned to somewhat normal. Jim cried out again,

"Jesus … Jesus. Help, help, and please help me. Jesus, please grant me strength."

The soft, gentle, nurturing voice spoke to Jim once again, saying, "Jim, may the peace of Jesus be with you, as the love of God is with you always. You know the Word of God; all of his children do. He has instilled it and wrote it on your heart; now speak the Word and know that it is true."

Although, the voice had spoken peace and love to Jim, he did not receive it as he had ten minutes ago. The agony was still upon his body and began attacking his mind and filling it with thoughts of defeat, death, suicide, anger, rejection, and destruction. In agony, Jim screamed, "In the name of Jesus, depart from me, you evil beings not of God. Every knee shall bow, and every tongue shall confess that Jesus is Lord. God's Word is true, and you must submit, for you are defeated, and you must depart from me now!"

There was a slight shriek that came from his head, almost like that of a startled rabbit, but it left immediately. All the symptoms that Jim had experienced were no longer present, as bountiful peace and love filled his body once again—God's love.

10

Jim arrived at his grandmother's house and noticed, as usual, an empty driveway. He never understood how she ran all her errands without a vehicle when she was at least three miles away from the closest bus stop. He revved the engine and swiftly accelerated as he pulled up to the garage.

A dim light shone through the side windows of the door of the house. Jim strode toward the door and rang the doorbell. Within a few minutes, his grandmother turned on the outside light and opened the door. "Jimmy, oh my goodness! It has been way too long. Come here and give your Grandma a hug!" She wrapped her arms around Jim and squeezed.

"It's good to see you too, Grandma. So, how's dinner?"

"Well, Jimmy boy, you were always impatient, wanting everything right then and there. As usual, you are going to have to wait. Come inside and sit on the couch."

She gestured Jim inside, followed after him, and closed the door. Jim plopped down on the couch and said, "Grandma, it sure smells good. Please don't tell me it's going to take too much longer. I can't wait to dig in and enjoy. I'm starved!"

"Jimmy, you need to hold your horses and just wait a minute."

Jim sat twiddling his thumbs and tapping his right foot. Two minutes, five minutes, and eventually ten minutes passed. Every passing moment seemed like a lifetime.

When the doorbell suddenly chimed, Jim perked his head up and looked at the door, concerned. "Um, Grandma, you want me to get that?"

"Yes, please. Dinner's almost done, so let them inside. Make sure that y'all wash up and sit at the dinner table."

"Um, Grandma, who else did you invite over? And do you want me to set the table?"

"Jimmy, you don't need to set the table. Don't worry about who I invited over. Just go see for yourself."

Jim rose from the couch as the doorbell rang a second time. He approached the door cautiously. Jim peeped through the peephole and smiled with glee. He swung open the door, saying, "Well, I'll be a monkey's uncle! What are you guys doing here?" There stood three familiar faces—James Andros, Kyle Rodd, and George Sights, his buddies from high school. Each gave a firm handshake followed by a hug.

James chuckled and asked, "Dude, where have you been, and why don't you keep in contact anymore? Last we heard from you, it was, like, six months ago."

Jim replied, "Well, you know, here and there. I've been bummed out with this whole economy bull-corn situation that's been going 'round. I have just tried to lie low and not spend any money. You know how it is."

James replied, "Well, man, all you gotta do is just give me a call. If you needed work, I could have talked with my uncle Jim Bob. He is still doing construction and would be more than happy to hook me up with a favor if I asked."

From the background, Carlene called out, "Are y'all boys just gonna sit there all night with my door open? I would most certainly proclaim that y'all were not raised in a barn. If y'all wait any longer, you're not gonna get hot food, so come in and wash up."

George smirked and chuckled. "Well, I don't know about you guys, but I'm going to eat. I have had the most tiring and intriguing day. If I don't eat, I will starve and pass out."

For as long as Jim could remember, George always had been a "one-upper." This meant that regardless of any circumstance or situation anyone was involved in, George's situation was always more embellished.

Jim quickly cut off George and said, "Trust me; this is one for the books. You guys probably won't believe me. Just wait until we get some food in our bellies, and I will explain everything." He gestured the three invited guests in and directed and followed them into the bathroom to wash up. They quickly washed their hands and then sat down at the dinner table.

"Well, about time," Carlene said. "I was beginning to think you boys didn't want to eat." She placed a pitcher of freshly brewed sweet tea in the center of the table and then returned to the kitchen to grab the rest of the food. The aroma of fresh cornbread, mashed potatoes, and pot roast with baby carrots filled the air.

"Grandma, you weren't kidding when you said you made too much for yourself. I sure am glad you called."

Carlene smiled gleefully and said, "Now, everybody, you just serve yourselves. Get as much as you want. There is plenty to go around."

Within seconds, food was piled on the plates, and the pitcher of tea was passed around the table. Once their plates were full, everyone glanced at each other and then back at Carlene.

"Well, are you hungry or what?" she asked. "It's not gonna bite you, so dig in!"

They all ate their fill and leaned back into the chairs with a sigh of relief. George glared at Jim until Jim turned and locked eyes with George. There was a brief moment of silence until George changed his expression to an artificial smile and a small chuckle. "So, Jim, what was this big story that happened to you today? It better be good, because I have something interesting myself that I would like to tell you guys."

Jim remained expressionless and gave another sigh before he explained the events that had occurred this day. He stopped the story when he got to the part where God gave him instructions to go to South America. He wondered where exactly in South America he was supposed to go. He had no idea of how he was going to get there or what he was supposed to do when he arrived. "Well, you see, God surprisingly chose me to go somewhere." Jim made sure that he gave extreme care to the wording he used. "I just don't know what I'm going to do when I get there, how I'm supposed to get there, or what."

A soft voice spoke to Jim. *Jim, why do you always lose faith so easily? Your Father has told you to do something. How is it that he would not provide fully?* A confused expression came over Jim until he realized that it was the Holy Spirit talking to him.

Throughout the story, George seemed quite edgy and studied each of Jim's comments.

Before Jim could continue his story, Carlene said, "Well, Jim, this is quite odd and funny that you mention it. I have something to give you." With that, she handed him a small white envelope. "I was going to give this to you a little later ... but now feels like the right time." She urged him to open it.

Jim carefully opened the envelope and removed a folded piece of paper. Jim exchanged a look with his grandmother and then focused his attention back on the paper. He slowly unfolded the it and began reading. His name was on the paper, followed by *Escape* and *Valid for one of the following: Venezuela, Jamaica, or Alaska.* "Grandma, what is this for, exactly?"

"Jimmy, don't you even remember that your birthday is next week? I decided to get you an early birthday present. I bought it a few months ago. There was a special on a new cruise liner. Just give them a call and tell them which you want."

George rolled his eyes in aggravation. His fingernails dug into his palm as he clenched his fist until his knuckles turned white. Jim looked at George and wondered what he was thinking. When George saw Jim looking at him, he relaxed. James and Kyle stared at Jim and laughed hysterically.

"Jim, you must be crazy," Kyle said. "You are an awesome storyteller. You should write short stories. I must say, though, that if that story were real …" Kyle trailed off and said nothing.

James said, "Thank you for the delicious food. We need to get going, as it is getting a little late. Thank you so much, Ms. Carlene."

"Aw, thank you so much, James. You boys are very welcome. I guess I will see you later, so until next time, y'all behave, okay? Jimmy, please show them out."

Jim walked his friends to the door, as James, Kyle, and George rubbed their stomachs contently. "All right, guys, until next time, I guess. It was good to see you."

"It really was nice to see you, Jim. Just please don't be a stranger. Give me a call so we can go out and have a good time, just like old times," said James.

"You're right, James. I will give you guys a call. I just need to find a job first and get the cash rolling in. I just may have to take you up on your offer about working with your uncle Jim Bob. I will call and schedule a luncheon or something to that effect."

With that, James, Kyle, and George got in James' car and backed out of the driveway. Everyone waved as George drove off and honked his horn twice.

Jim returned to the kitchen, where he found his grandmother almost done cleaning up. "Grandma, do you believe me?"

"Jim, of course I do. That story was too intricate to be fabricated. Besides, I don't believe in coincidences, such as purchasing that cruise line ticket for your birthday. I know that they leave next week. Be sure to call them first thing in the morning to set yourself up for a guaranteed seat."

"I will, Grandma. Grandma, I have something else to ask you. Today was crazy, completely mind-boggling. It caused me to reminisce on the past, back to when Dad died. Everything is hazy, and I don't remember what happened to Dad and Shaun."

Carlene was taken aback. She took a deep breath and fought off her tears. Her words were muffled until she cleared her throat to speak. "Jim, that day was so terrible. I try to block it out and forget about it. It was raining that day, and a lady with two toddlers was broken down on the side of a two–lane road. Several cars pulled over to help, with various men attempting to fix the situation. Your dad insisted on pulling over. The lady had her car facing another to get a jump. There were three cars behind her car and five cars behind the car facing hers. Your dad always liked to fix things and went between the two vehicles to look at what was going on."

Carlene had to stop talking for a brief moment as tears rolled down her cheeks. Her voice began to crack, and her words became mumbled as she said, "It was entirely his fault. That man decided to drink and drive. It was bad enough that it was raining … and to throw alcohol in the mix to have a good time … It was dark and the roads were slick. He was speeding and slammed on his brakes. His car slid sixty feet and lost traction on the road. The car turned ninety degrees and continued sliding. His car slammed into the last car and caused a chain reaction until it smashed your father like a pancake."

Carlene was on the verge of an emotional breakdown but forced herself to continue. "Everyone panicked. Your father still managed to hold on to a threshold of life as the cars were removed, and he fell to the ground. Shaun did everything he could to keep your dad awake, but your father had sporadic blackouts. The EMT personnel arrived on the scene twelve minutes later and took your father to the emergency room."

"Grandma, I am still unclear about one thing. Was Shaun in the paramedics' vehicle with Dad? I don't remember seeing him at the hospital."

"That's just it, Jimmy. He never made it to the hospital. From what I understand, he disappeared just prior to the EMT's arrival. Some believe that out of anger and shock, he took off and ran away. We filed a missing persons report after your father died, but we've never heard from him since then." Carlene's eyes were full of tears, and she could no longer speak. Her mascara ran down her cheeks and trickled off her chin. She hunched over and slowly rocked herself.

Jim wondered why he didn't remember any of this. It was his life, after all, so shouldn't he have remembered something this significant? He knew that this event held a significant role in the events that followed and had to be a clue as to what was occurring now. Jim knelt down and held his grandmother to comfort her. No words were spoken until she stopped crying and wiped her tears away.

"Thank you, Jimmy. I think I'm going to turn in for the night. I love you."

"Don't worry, Grandma. I have a strong sense that everything is going to be made known soon enough. I love you too, Grandma." With that, Jim returned to his house. His head swirled with thoughts of what might occur. He began talking continuously to God, asking aloud what he was to do and questioning why God had chosen him. He lay his head down on his pillow, slowly blinking.

11

Jim lay in his bed, tossing and turning as he became more and more restless. Visions from the past entered his mind as he attempted to shut his eyes more firmly. He counted forward to twenty-five and then backward. He thought, "When is this going to end? God, I don't know if I can accomplish what you desire of me. Just look at my past history and where I came from. How can you possibly use a person like me, one who has gone to the edge of humanity, and use him to better your goal? I do not pretend that I know how I am going to succeed or why this is happening. How do I know if you are even listening to me? I never hear you respond."

Jim took a deep breath and then exhaled. Once again, he began his conversation with God. "Well, how is this going to end? The Bible was written centuries ago, and that was only through word of mouth. How can I convince people that this is real? How am I to communicate with people if I cannot even speak a lick of Spanish or Portuguese or any other language apart from English?"

Jim shifted his weight and turned onto his stomach. He slid both arms under the pillow and rested his chin on top of the pillow. "Well, Lord, I am going to do this that you have tasked me with. I just have one question for you, and I ask that you please show this to me, so that I may fully know why I am doing this. You said you are going to return to earth in the clouds and take up your people. I know this as the rapture. How is the rapture going to happen, and who is going? What would happen if I were led astray or backslid, like the Bible says?"

Immediately following Jim's conversation and prayer with God, he fell into a deep sleep and awoke in a dream.

A stern yet familiar voice spoke to Jim, saying, "You have asked the Father to show you this, and so you shall know how it ends. You will not know the time or date. You could try asking a person, but even then, your brain would not process this information. You will remember this entirely, as it will be imbedded into your brain like a past memory."

Jim looked up and all around the room. "Great. Now I have been suddenly transported to … back to my room? Who is this speaking? I can hear you, but I still don't know where you are"

"Must we go through these building blocks of questions? Jim, I have already explained to you that I am an angel and therefore not limited to the laws of mankind for I am limited to the laws that our Father has set."

"Asrel, don't tell me that's you. You drop me off at my house and whammo, you are now here in my … let me guess—another dream, right?"

"Yes, Jim, you are correct once more in your questions, but once again, I am limited to the amount of knowledge that I am permitted to reveal. I must go."

Asrel left without another word, and Jim was left to his ponder his thoughts. "All right, so I'm in a dream. I wonder if I can do cool things, like defy gravity. Oh, better yet, I've always wanted to try pinching myself and see if it works. Here goes nothing." Jim pinched the soft, delicate skin under his left arm—and the pain there was real.

"Man, what the crap is this? What kind of dream is this? I've always thought I could do anything in a dream and not feel pain."

Another firm yet familiar voice spoke then. "Jim, get up out of bed and go forward."

Nothing else was said as Jim obeyed willingly and without question. He quickly stretched and exited his bedroom. Jim found himself outside in the scorching sun.

Jim scoped his surroundings in an attempt to see where he was. He could see gloomy clouds in the distance and knew that the clouds would soon engulf the sun. Several minutes passed and it looked like it was about to rain. He noticed a long road and a convenience store located within walking distance. Behind the convenience store were green pastures, blocked off by barbed wire. Cattle roamed the pastures and grazed as they pleased. People walked in and out of the convenience store, carrying bags of purchased items.

They walked through a parking lot and passed a strip mall of stores. Several cars passed to and fro on the street, and some turned into the parking lot. Jim began walking to the convenience store. He had a strong urge to go there to see why it was so popular.

When he arrived at the store, he blatantly disregarded what Asrel had said; he asked the first person he saw for the date and time. As the person spoke, his words became jumbled, and all Jim could hear was noise—a noise that was like a billion people talking at the same time, all in different languages. It was impossible to understand what he was saying at that moment, so Jim didn't worry about it. The convenience store had nothing unusual about it, so Jim decided to walk back outside. He would then began looking for any kind of sign from God that might direct him either way. Jim stepped outside and folded his arms, with his right hand to his chin, attempting to think which way to go first.

A loud rumble came from the horizon. Jim believed a stampede of crazed animals was heading his way. He slightly squatted in an attempt to hold his balance and prepare for the worst—he didn't know that the worst was soon to come. Jim's eyes darted everywhere in search of this stampede.

There was a loud exploding noise that came from the sky. The noise was very loud and was could be heard by all. Jim's heart sank to the pit of his stomach as the Scripture unfolded in his mind and heart. The noise sounded like a strange trumpet, but when the sound blasted again, Jim could hear words being said. The words sounded like a symphonic choir, saying in unison, "Rejoice for the King of Kings has returned to take you away from the hour of infamy."

Jim looked at all the people and noticed that some had dropped to their knees, crying in agony, and some were running to the pastures. All were looking up. Jim looked where they were running and found a ray of light on a small patch of grass in the pastures. Jim looked up and noticed that a great cloud was rolling like a tumbling ball. The cloud was white and acted as if it were a chariot for one rider. A man stood on top of the cloud, wearing a crown. Although the man was in the distance, he was large enough that all could see him.

Every time the man spoke, his words were written in the clouds in crimson red. "For those who have waited in good faith, arise." Billions of balls of light, no bigger than the size of an orange, all shot up from the ground and simultaneously went to the man on the cloud.

I know you; I know that I must know you, Jim thought, and it hit him like an upper cut. *The man standing on the cloud and the "King of Kings" can only mean one thing. The man who is known by many names is … is … Jesus.*

"Arise, all you who have known me and have their names written in the Lamb's Book of Life."

There were only a few, from what Jim could tell, who had gone up to Jesus as fast as the speed of light. To many other individuals, this would seem as if they just vanished into thin air. The only thing that remained was what was on their persons, such as clothes, shoes, jewelry, hair accessories, and eyeglasses. All the articles fell simultaneously with a small thud. Still, there were those who were running to the pastures.

Jim knew that he had to go. He didn't want to get left behind, after all. He bolted across the street and jumped right over the barbed-wire fence. Jim passed individuals left and right as he sprinted. This was no mere race to Jim; it was his only chance. He knew that if he couldn't catch up to Jesus and cry out, he wouldn't make it. He would be left behind, just like the multitude.

Jim made it to the ray of light and began jumping up in the air. Only for a moment did he feel like he was floating. This moment was full of tranquility—until he came crashing down. Jim landed hard, flat on his back, knocking the wind from his lungs temporarily. While lying there, Jim noticed nearly thirty-five people around him. They were on their knees with their hands clasped and their faces toward the heavens, crying out, saying, "Lord, Lord, please have mercy on me. Pity me, Lord. Don't forget about all my good deeds. I was a good person."

Many were crying aloud, begging to be taken up. Still, Jim could not speak or move; all he could do was look up. Jim saw Jesus, with tears streaming down his cheeks. Then he turned his head and gritted his teeth. "You have never known me, nor have you ever offered me a drink of water. I do not know you. Away from me, you wicked and perverse generation." Just like that, he left the way he had come. The cloud rolled back into itself, and the clouds became gloomy once more.

To Jim's amazement, it only took thirteen seconds for this entire process to happen. Everything seemed in slow-motion and on fast-forward at the same time. The air returned to Jim's lungs, and he took a deep breath. He began to cry, as did everyone else. He'd missed his shot, the only shot he had to get out of this place. It was foretold and prophesied many centuries ago. Instead of listening to what God had said, he had chosen to enjoy his time here. Jim was forced to stop mid-thought when a screeching and whirring sound came from above.

Explosions came from every which way. Jim's gut reaction was to get out of the area immediately. He tried to run, but his legs were wobbly from landing flat on his back. The noise coming from above grew louder and louder, forcing Jim's attention upward. It took only a moment for Jim to say, "Jesus, please save me …"

Just then, a Boeing 747 began to crush Jim's body.

Jim then awoke in amazement in his bed. He looked at the alarm clock and saw it was only 2:25. "Phew! It was only a dream." Parched, Jim arose from his bed and went to the kitchen. The house was pitch-black, save for a few patches of moonlight shining through the windows. Jim was looking down, attempting to open his eyes. He was near the end of the hallway that separated the walkway and the kitchen. In the middle of the archway was a pair of feet. Jim's eyes shot wide open, and he darted his eyes to see the individual's face. The person had his back turned to Jim, and he turned before Jim could say a word.

"You wanted to talk to our Father, so you can talk to me."

Once again, Jim dropped to his knees and cried out, "Forgive me, Lord. I am unworthy."

"Jim, I told you that you were forgiven. Once again, please arise."

Jim was quivering and almost in a state of shock. His experience from the dream was almost too much. Panting for breath, he stood upright and slowly began to speak. "Lord, it is all too much. I just didn't know how to explain to anyone what was happening. These dreams that I have are testing my limits. I don't know if I can go on."

"God will never give you anything that you cannot withstand. He has all knowledge and wisdom. If you believe your yoke to be too great, just lean unto me, for my yoke is not great."

Jim thought wisely what he should say to Jesus. "Lord, if I had not visited you earlier and accepted you, what would have happened to me?"

"Had you continued in the same course that you were on, you would not have been able to be with me or our Father. I have told a generation of this secret, but they denied it. I told them that wide is the gate to hell and narrow is the road to heaven. Salvation is the only key to finding the small and narrow. You would have found yourself in a terrible situation that could never be undone."

The moonlight reflected off the wall and cast a dim light in the hallway. Jim was only able to decipher what Jesus looked like. He looked different here in this state.

"Jim, your task is set ahead. Although our Father knows what you are about to do, I tell you to refrain from doing so. Fulfill your set task, and do not stray. Doing so will cause you to act as past prophets have done, and you shall partake of the same ordeals they have undergone. I tell you the truth. The Father has told me that soon I will return. It is his elect that are slowing down the process. They pray to lengthen the time frame and stray from his will. I can assure you that I shall return within your lifetime, and the time is very near. Now awake and go forth."

Just as directed, Jim fell backwards, and his eyelids started to feel heavy. Jim became unable to move and began to breathe deeply and rhythmically until he fell into unconsciousness.

12

Jim awoke to a nagging alarm clock, the type that never seemed
to snooze and always became louder. Blinking his eyes, he rolled
over and slammed his hand against the alarm clock. The time
was 5:03 a.m. Feeling groggy and lazy, Jim closed his eyes and
enjoyed the relaxation. Just as he was about to fall asleep, a voice
reverberated from the back of his mind, saying, "Go forth."

He sat up in his bed, inhaled deeply, and then yawned and
rubbed his eyes. He grunted as he slid his legs off the bed and flexed
his toes on the carpet. Standing up, Jim stretched thoroughly and
yawned again and walked to the bathroom. Looking in the mirror,
he began examining himself for signs of aging.

This daily ritual usually began and ended with staring at the
mirror—Jim considered this a form of self-preservation. The ritual
was lengthy but allowed Jim time to do a daily checklist of chores
or errands as he stared in the mirror. Still feeling groggy, it took a
moment for his brain to warm up.

Jim closed his eyes and visualized a piece of college-ruled
writing paper. He then visualized writing down his tasks for the
day, beginning with this morning ritual—Jim then checked off this
task. Scanning his memory, he contemplated what else he needed
to do. He remembered that he needed to call Escape Cruise Liner.
Jim added this to the list, and with that, he stopped making a list.

Jim brushed his teeth, and then returned to his bedroom to gather the cruise voucher. He read through the restrictions and found the number to make a reservation. Jim went to the kitchen to make the call. When his call was answered, he was put on hold and listened to several different genres of music, as well as a female voice occasionally saying, "Thank you for choosing Escape Cruise Liner. We are happy to serve you at any hour. All of our representatives are responding to other customers. Please hold, and you will be served in the order the call was made."

Several minutes passed, during which Jim became anxious. Bored, tired, and a little groggy, he began tapping his right foot. His left eye began to twitch, and he randomly scratched it.

He heard a clicking noise on the other end of the phone, and then another female voice said, "Hello, this is Ashley with Escape Cruise Liner. Whom do I have the pleasure of helping today?"

Jim took a deep breath and said excitedly, "Hello Ashley, my name is Jim Ackelson. My grandmother purchased a gift voucher for me, and I would like to see what options you have available."

Ashley asked for the confirmation number and then informed Jim, "The packages available with that voucher are to Jamaica, Alaska, or Hawaii."

"Ashley, could you see if there's a cruise to South America. I was really hoping to go there; I hear it is amazing."

"Yes, sir … Mr. Ackelson, it says that there is only one seat available, and it is set to take off tomorrow to Venezuela. The seat was reserved by another customer who just canceled. The seat is in first class and costs $236.48. Would you like to book this itinerary?"

Jim remembered that some of his bills were due so he decided against it. Jim sighed in disappointment and said, "I just can't afford that right now. I would, however, like to book an itinerary to Jamaica."

There was muffled typing in the background, and then Ashley said, "Mr. Ackelson, you can depart from Mayport, Florida, in two weeks—or you can depart tomorrow morning at eight o'clock from Panama City, Florida."

Without hesitation, Jim chose the second option.

"Is there anything else that I may assist you with today Mr. Ackelson?" Ashley asked.

"No, ma'am, you have been awesome," Jim answered.

He was ecstatic that he would be able to escape from this place, even if only for a week. Immediately, he dialed James' number. After a few rings, James' groggy voice answered the phone. When he realized it was Jim, he said, "Man what time is it? Jim, are you seriously calling me at 7:04 in the morning? Are you on crack or something? What is so important that you needed to wake me?"

"Bro, I got some awesome news, but I have a favor that I need to ask you."

James scoffed, "You're a funny guy. You honestly have to be kidding me. Let me guess—you want to stay over, like old times. Better yet, you want some money, right?"

"Come on, James, why are you being like this? You never act like this. I can expect remarks like that from George. Will you just please listen to me and what I have to say?"

James tried to clear his head and attempted to not get upset because he'd been awoken so early. "I'm sorry, Jim. I didn't sleep well last night. I had some crazy dreams that seemed entirely too realistic. I think it was because of the story you told us last night over dinner. I can't explain it; it's mind-boggling. Sorry about ranting. I just got a little excited. So what is it you need?"

"Hey, bro, it's no problem. I was wondering if you could drive me to Panama City, Florida, early in the morning. I just claimed the gift voucher and booked myself for a cruise leaving tomorrow to Jamaica. The thing is, I just don't trust my car to make the trip to Panama City. If you are able and willing, I need a ride down."

"I don't have anything planned, so yeah, I can take you. Besides, it may give us some time to catch up. What time?"

"I need to be there by 8:00 a.m., so we will need to leave here around six."

"All right, Jim. I will pick you up about ten 'til five so we can have enough time to drive there. I will see you in the morning and I'm going to go back to sleep now."

"I appreciate it, man, and I will see you first thing in the morning."

Jim hung up the phone and began to gather the things he would need for a week-long trip. Excitement ran through his veins, and each heartbeat caused a tingling sensation in the pit of his stomach. Jim continued to pack throughout the day, and as the day dwindled down to dusk, Jim knew that he probably would be too excited to sleep. He had to awaken early, though, so Jim decided it was best to try to go to sleep early.

13

A nagging sound in Jim's room upset him. He was in a light sleep, almost awake but still asleep, but there was that annoying sound. Jim knew what he had to do, but his body fought against his mind. Lying there, Jim contemplated his options: return to his sleep; shut off the alarm clock and return to sleep; or face the obvious and start his day. He lay there listening to the nagging alarm clock and continued to fade in and out of sleep.

Jim remained motionless for the next several minutes—until his house phone rang. The house phone had a higher pitch than his annoying alarm clock and almost always seemed to startle him. This might have been because people rarely called him, save the bill collectors. Jim did not hate the bill collectors; he just hated the fact that people called his house at weird hours and told him that he owed them money. Who in their right mind liked to owe a debt to a person? As he shut off his alarm clock and made his way to the phone, Jim thought back to when he began accumulating mounds of debt.

The first memory was when he finished high school and was out at the mall. The mall—coincidentally the same mall as in the dream he'd had earlier that week—was where it started. He walked through Macy's and signed up for in-store credit. There were numerous clothing items that he wanted. He'd always dreamed of making it big in the world and believed that he needed dress clothes to achieve success. With a deep sigh, Jim quit thinking about what he owed as he picked up the receiver.

He cleared his throat and groggily answered, "Hello. Who is it, and why are you calling so early?"

"Jim-my, it's time to wake up, my brotha," replied an indistinct voice.

"Who is calling me, and why is it time to get up?"

"Jim, you really don't know who is calling? Man, you must have really not slept last night. It's James. I'm calling you to ensure that you are up and to let you know that I will be there in about five minutes."

"Oh wow, it really is that early and time to go already. All right, I am going to leave the door unlocked for you and go get ready."

Feeling a little dazed and still somewhat exhausted, Jim slammed the receiver down and then rushed to the front door, unlocked it, and ran back to the bathroom to make a hasty morning routine. It felt like only seconds since he'd hung up the phone when he heard James enter the front door.

"Jimmy, we gotta head out within ten minutes if we are going to make our deadline," called James.

Jim finished his morning ritual in one-eighth of the time as usual and threw on a pair of jeans, a blue T-shirt, socks, and a pair of tennis shoes. He grabbed his luggage and walked briskly to the living room, where James awaited.

"Bro, what took you so long? You are cutting it close today, as we have two minutes to spare. Luckily, I thought of getting driving directions and input the information in my GPS. So we just need to get you loaded in my car and bounce."

"Everything is packed and ready to go," Jim said. "I just need to lock my front door, and we will be well on our way. I know it's a bad question to ask you, but since I just woke up, is there any possible way that we can get some food or something?"

"Well, I took the liberty of bringing you two cinnamon rolls and a thing of apple juice."

Jim ushered James to the door with his luggage. He shut off the thermostat and turned off the light in all the rooms before he returned to the front door. Jim looked for his luggage, but James had already loaded it in his car. Jim locked the door and jogged to the James' white Chevrolet Malibu.

As Jim got in the car, James offered him the cinnamon rolls and a small carton of apple juice. James then pulled out of Jim's driveway and made his way to Panama City. Every bite that Jim took was sensational and delicious; the rolls practically melted in his mouth. Once he finished the cinnamon rolls, Jim polished off the carton of apple juice and let out a sigh of relief. "James, I really hate to do this to you; I feel really guilty about it, but I honestly don't know if I can stay awake. I know you got up early because of me, but I really did not get any sleep last night."

"Eh, don't sweat it, man. I had a couple cups of coffee. Go ahead and take a nap. I promise to wake you up when we get there."

"Thank you, James, you are an awesome brother that anyone would be jealous to have." Jim reclined his seat, blinked a few times, and fell asleep.

As promised, James woke Jim when they reached Panama City. Jim inhaled deeply, stretched, and then returned his seat in the upright position. He looked out the window and noticed that they were by the pier and a large cruise liner. A metal assembly connected to the liner so that people could make their way to the deck of the ship. Several people seemed to showing their itineraries to the staff and making their way on board.

"James, you really are a life saver, bro. I don't know where I would be without you."

"It's no problem, man. You know that you can ask me for anything you need at any time. You had better get going because I don't want you to miss your vacation." James chuckled as they got out of the Malibu, and James opened the trunk and handed Jim his luggage.

They embraced each other with a firm hug and then shook hands. "All right, I guess that means you're good to go. Just remember not to do anything that I wouldn't do," James said, chuckling slightly as he returned to his Malibu.

"Well, James, when I get back, I suppose I will be a new man who is fully rested. Again, I can't express my gratitude enough. Have a safe trip home." Jim waved at James and turned to walk up to the liner. James honked his horn as he drove off to the freeway.

There was a security terminal at the pier, just prior to walking up the ramp. Jim was astonished that TSA even provided services for cruise liners, but then again. He understood that security was paramount nowadays. Jim placed his luggage and shoes in a plastic tray.

The tray moved forward on the conveyor belt and passed through a machine to be screened. Jim stopped in front of the metal detector and waited to be prompted to move forward. The TSA employee gestured to Jim, and he passed through the metal detector with ease. He collected his belongings, put on his shoes, and continued forward to the metal ramp.

Employees asked if anyone needed a hand toting their luggage up the metal ramp. Jim knew that it was customary to tip the person who helped, and he couldn't really afford it. Jim carried his own luggage, but he had, as usual, packed light.

Still, the walk caused Jim to break a mild sweat. He met the employee checking for the proper itinerary. Jim grabbed the paper with the confirmation code and handed it to the employee. With everything in order, the employee allowed Jim to come aboard. The employee gave Jim a boarding pass, a list of event times and locations, and the card key for his room.

People were walking about in every direction. Jim noticed an elevator with a vaulted ceiling of glass windows. The walls were white, and the floor was made of marble. There were people of all ages and different ethnicities. Jim was quite pleased with this gift, as several beautiful young women walked in a group, laughing aloud.

Jim raised both eyebrows and had a sly smile. In the attempt to not gawk at the young women, Jim focused on his boarding pass and checked his room number—room 831.

Jim looked around for an indication of his location and saw a large map of the ship on the wall in front of him. He walked to the map and realized that he was on the main deck and then that his room was located seven decks below.

He took the elevator to the eighth floor. Interesting enough, there were no people in the elevator with him. As the elevator doors opened, he saw a sign with arrows pointed in opposite directions. Rooms 800 to 850 were to the left; rooms 851 to 899 were to the right. Jim's room was ten feet from the elevator, on the right side of the hallway.

Jim inserted his card key in the door's electronic switch. The machine beeped twice, and a small green light signaled to Jim that the door was unlocked.

14

A foghorn blasted in the distance and was followed by music and cheers. Jim placed his luggage on the floor near the door and went to the porthole to see the commotion. While looking through the porthole, he felt a slight vibration and rocking sensation. Looking out at the pier, he noticed several people waving at the cruise liner. With a smile and chuckle, Jim closed the porthole and turned to inspect his room.

The room was small in comparison to his bedroom at home. There was a single bed, a dresser, a closet, a twenty-two-inch television mounted to the ceiling, a small desk, and a chair. There was also a bathroom with a stand-up shower, a toilet, and a sink with a mirror above it. Jim threw his luggage on top of the bed and began unpacking. He filled the dresser drawers in a segregated manner. The top draw was for socks and boxers, the second drawer was for shirts, the third drawer was for shorts, and the last drawer was for pants. Once finished unpacking, he placed the empty duffel bag and suitcase at the bottom of the closet.

He thought out loud, saying "It certainly is not bad for a week. I really don't think I will be here much, other than to sleep. I wonder what kind of attractions and entertainment they will have."

Searching through his pockets, Jim found the trifold brochure with the ship's event information and times. He scanned the front page of the brochure. *Escape Cruises: Your getaway destination to live, laugh, love, and to escape.*

Underneath the title of the brochure was a picture of people in a spotlight, smiling and dancing in evening gowns and suits. In the rear of the picture were tables with five-star quality gourmet meals. The people at the tables seemed to be conversing and laughing. Behind them, a band playing; the band members were wearing tuxedos.

Flipping the page, Jim found the meal times. *Breakfast: 6:00 a.m.–8:00 a.m.; Lunch: 11:00 a.m.–1:00 p.m.; Cocktails 4:00 p.m.– 5:00 p.m.; Dinner: 5:00 p.m.–7:00 p.m.; Evening Meal: 11:00 p.m.– 1:00 a.m.* The second page of the trifold brochure listed gambling times. *Texas Hold'em: all day, beginning every hour; Omaha: all day beginning every hour.* Underneath the list of card games was information on family games, such as Monopoly, Uno, Life, and Scene It.

There were additional games listed, but Jim stopped reading and skipped to the next page. This page listed dance lessons and types of dances that would be available throughout the day. The next page listed laundry and dry-cleaning times for each of the floors. Jim was quite impressed by the brochure and went to wash his face to begin his first day of his vacation.

Jim left his room with his wallet and card key in his pocket. He went to the elevator and pressed the letter "M" for mess deck. The doors closed and the elevator began to move up. Jim stepped to the back to lean against the railing.

Suddenly, an audible voice spoke to Jim. "Why have you disobeyed me? You shall soon understand that it is impossible to run away from the will of God. Take up the full armor of God and prepare yourself. The one you dream of knows where you are, and you shall soon enough be tested."

Jim attempted to argue with the voice, but Jim had cotton-mouth as soon as the voice spoke. He knew full well that he was in the wrong and should have trusted in God. He should have spent the money in his bank account on the trip to Venezuela. He knew that it was God who had spoken to him, and he feared what was to come.

The elevator came to a slow stop and opened the doors. Exiting the elevator, Jim scanned the room with many tables, each accommodating six people comfortably. The room was half filled. Some were eating lunch and others were waiting for their meals. Jim walked to a podium where a greeter in a tuxedo waited. He smiled at Jim. "Hello, sir, and welcome. Is there anyone else accompanying you on this wonderful day?"

"Uh, no, sir, it's just me today," Jim replied.

"You may have a seat anywhere you would like. Here is our lunch menu."

Jim took the menu and asked, "What would you recommend? I want to get something quite filling but not heavy on the calories, if you know what I mean."

"I am happy you asked that, sir. Everything on our menu has a medium- to low-calorie ratio. You can order a main entrée, followed by two sides and a dessert. You can also choose to have either a full portion or a half portion. Your waiter or waitress will be more than happy to help you with your order."

"Thank you," replied Jim. He went to the nearest table and sat down. Jim was in the mood for a medium-rare steak. He scanned the menu and decided that he also wanted a loaded sweet potato and seasonal vegetables, sweet tea, and a slice of carrot cake. Closing the menu Jim looked up and noticed that his waiter just arrived. "Hello, sir, I am Jerry, and I will be taking care of you for this meal. What can I get you to drink?"

"Hi, Jerry, I would like to order."

"What can I get for you today?"

"I would like a ten-ounce medium-rare steak with a loaded baked sweet potato, seasonal vegetables, and sweet tea. For dessert, I would like a slice of carrot cake."

"All right, sir, your order will be coming out shortly."

"Jerry, I am going to wash up. You can just leave the sweet tea, and I will get it when I get back, okay?"

"It's no problem, sir." Jerry turned and went to the kitchen to place Jim's order.

Jim walked to the men's room, which was decorated in beige tile on the floor and the top of the walls. The bottom of the walls had black marble that matched the counter. The sink and faucet were stainless steel, and the counter was lined with different articles, such as colognes, Q-Tips, mints, breath spray, towels, and a tip jar. An employee waited by the counter to offer any articles or suggestions. He wore a tuxedo, a pair of dark sunglasses, and a nametag that read "Richard."

"Hello, Richard," Jim said. "How much do you charge for a mint and a splash of cologne?"

"Nothing, sir, it's complimentary. Should you feel the need, you may tip, but if you don't care to tip, I just ask for a handshake." Richard then offered a cunning and devious smile.

Jim felt cautious around Richard. He felt a strange presence surrounding Richard. Jim never knew anyone who would accept a smile over a tip. Jim turned on the faucet and ran his hands under the stream of warm water; then he placed his hands on his face.

"Sir, I have towels for that if you would like." Richard had his hand extended with a towel. Jim took the towel and ran it under the stream of water. He wrung out the towel and placed the warm, damp towel on his head. He closed his eyes.

A few moments passed as Jim relaxed and then removed the towel. Richard showed Jim where to drop the towel and then offered Jim a dry towel to Jim.

"Thank you, Richard," Jim said. "It is much appreciated. I cannot really afford to tip you right now, and I do apologize. I can give you a smile and a handshake, though." Jim extended his hand to Richard, who smiled and clasped Jim's hand.

"Jim, I was hoping you would say that."

Astonished, Jim tried to retract his hand but was unable to do so.

The lights in the room began to flicker off and on. Each time was faster than the last, until they were standing in complete darkness. The room shook violently as it began to move. "Jim, I have been waiting a long time to talk to you. I'm here strictly on business—business that is of my Lord. I'm here to … let me say … to offer you a deal."

"Who are you and what do you want?" asked Jim.

"Oh, come now. We don't have all day to play games. You know who I work for. Let's just cut to the chase. I will accompany you on a little trip, which you cannot leave until I say so. You can do just about anything you want where we are going, though, so you might as well enjoy yourself."

God, can you please help me here? Jim thought. *Oh my goodness, what am I going to do?*

The room stopped moving, and the lights returned to normal. The bathroom was in the same condition as it had been a few moments ago. Richard let go of Jim's hand. Jim immediately turned and bolted toward the door, but when he burst through the door, he found himself in open air. The world seemed quite busy, as cars passed by on the freeway. People walked from shop to shop. Skyscrapers were scattered about.

Richard stood at Jim's side, smiling deviously. "Welcome to the future, Jim … or let me just say, of what this future could be for you." Richard began acting as a tour guide for Jim. "You see, everything is almost the same in this time. People are happier here, as we are disease-free. Our economy could never be better, as there are no unemployed citizens. Soon, in the near future, there will be a technological revolution that jump-starts the economy. The revolution will call for all to be in the workforce. Soon, after the initial breakthrough in technology, there will be a breakthrough in medical science. The trend will go forth to solve just about all of mankind's needs. People will desire to work, as they will receive all of these benefits in their packages. The task ahead will be difficult, should you decline this offer. The man I work for is quite brilliant and has done his research."

"Richard, I don't know what to tell you. This honestly sounds too good to be true, and you already know the saying—furthermore, people don't just want to work. Do you really take me for a fool? I went from having everything on the brink of ruins, all the way to everything being hunky dory. I see that people are happier here, and I see that there is a significant change, but what is the cost and what is the scheme? Nobody ever cut me a break in life, so why would your boss decide that now is as good as any to toss me a bone? I have seen only what is in front of me. What else is there to see?"

Richard laughed and replied, "I'm glad you asked. There is honestly too much to show you in this one visit. So let's go to your personal office. I really think you are going to like it. It's located in downtown Safensburg, New York."

"Wait a minute—Safensburg? I have never heard of a city named Safensburg, New York."

Richard raised his hand for a nearby cab. The cab stopped and picked up Richard and Jim.

"Good day, Mr. Ackelson and Mr. Caudwell," replied the cab driver.

"Good day, Mr. Ecks. Please take us to Mr. Ackelson's office."

Mr. Ecks nodded and drove to central Safensburg, New York and Richard continued talking to Jim.

"As I said, Jim, this is what the future could be, should you decide so. There were issues among the nations that caused another world war to break out. Instead of two factions, there were four factions against each other. Some cities were decimated. Each faction aimed warheads at the others and were cautious to any movement or inclination. The standstill between the factions was three times worse than the Cold War with the United States and Russia. There was a catastrophic catalyst as people began disappearing. Each faction blamed the other for espionage and assassination. Although there was no actual proof, they fired upon each other, killing almost a billion of the world's population. It did not end until my boss took charge and delivered us into this era of peace and tranquility. You helped him deliver the world from its original chaotic state and implement the technology needed to remain constant."

Mr. Ecks came to a stop in front of the largest skyscraper in the city. The base of the skyscraper was three city blocks in length. Several people in suits were walking and talking on some new type of Bluetooth device. The first floor of the skyscraper was full of tinted glass.

"How about we head inside your building, Jim?" Richard said.

Inside the building was a thirteen-foot security desk with four sentries posted around it, wearing white uniforms.

To the right of the security unit was a lobby with several massage recliners, a table with magazines, and couches. Behind the security unit was the receptionist area, where two receptionists were seated. Jim and Richard passed through a metal detector and walked past the security guards who greeted them. They proceeded toward the elevators that were just past the reception area.

"Good morning, Mr. Ackelson. Good morning, Mr. Ecks. Here is your coffee." The receptionist handed them each a coffee cup.

Jim and Richard entered the elevator and headed to the top floor. The top floor was magnificent. The room had mahogany walls and marble floors. Chandeliers hung from the ceiling with diamonds. A receptionist sat near two French-style doors with the words "Jim Ackelson" engraved on them. Jim smiled but raised his eyebrows with suspicion.

"Hello, Mr. Ackelson. It is good to see you today. You have an appointment in five minutes with the boss and another appointment with Anthony Litchel at eleven thirty to discuss further biometric research and implementation," said Jeannine.

"Thank you … Jeannine. You say five minutes with the boss?" Jim asked in a confused manner.

"Yes, sir, he said it was urgent, so I hope you are prepared," replied Jeannine.

More than you know, Jim thought.

Richard and Jim entered the office. Jim had a workout machine, a putter machine, all types of video games, a sixty-inch flat-screen TV facing his desk, and several leather couches. His desk was made of cedar and had a high-gloss finish. Jim sat in his recliner that served as his personal work chair.

"I can't wait until you talk to the boss," Richard said. "He is by far the greatest man I have ever known. I am sure you will like him; everyone adores him." Richard sat on a nearby couch. Jim sat in his recliner, taking in the room and his so-called near future.

A voice spoke inside his head: "Take up the full armor of God." No more and no less was said.

A buzzer sounded at the corner of Jim's neatly organized desk. "Mr. Ackelson, the boss is waiting on the TV for you. Turn it on to channel 63 for a video conference."

Jim found the remote in the top center drawer of his desk. He turned on the TV and flipped to channel 63. To Jim's surprise, the man had dark and light brown hair. He had no wrinkles or blemishes on his face; he had a baby face. He was well shaven, with light eyebrows and eyelashes and light blue eyes.

The man wore a three-piece gray suit, white shirt, and a red silk tie. He sat upright, with his hands clasped together, and wore a white-gold ring with a ruby center on his right pinky finger. Jim began to shake and tremble; he tried to doubt what was blatantly obvious. This was the man who had haunted him in his dreams. This was the guy he could never escape. This was the guy who always laughed at and mocked him. This was the guy. This was the Antichrist.

15

Jim sat in his chair with a show of strength and might, withholding any sign of fear. Light sweat trickled down his forehead on either side. Jim crossed his legs at his ankle and clasped his hands in his lap. The Antichrist had an arrogant smile. He sat in a leather office chair with reserved authority, in a calm, cool, and collected manner. He radiated strength and power, even through the TV.

"Hello, Jim. I have been waiting to speak with you for some time now. I take it that Richard has shown you around a bit. So tell me, do you like your office and the things that you have heard and seen?"

Jim hesitated before speaking, as he tried to phrase his words properly. "Who are you? Why have you chosen me and why have you shown me these things?" asked Jim.

The Antichrist cocked his head. "I suppose you are correct. We are due for proper introductions. Jim, I have known you, and you have known me all your life. Things have most certainly changed since our last encounter. My name has changed several times with each avenue and victory in my life. I have studied generously and have worked diligently for what you now see. I can't take full credit for everything, of course, as my master has aided me, as have you, of course. I cherish him and do anything he asks of me. There was a brief moment in time, however, when I went by the name of Shaun. Does any of this surprise you?"

Jim unclasped his hands and placed them on his desk. He squinted his eyes and narrowed his eyebrows as he rapped his fingertips on top of the desk. "I don't know any Shaun's so that is irrelevant to me. I suppose since you won't tell me your real name that I shall refer to you as Shaun. There are too many things that I just don't get. How? How did you come up with all of this? This society is all too perfect, and mankind is not perfect. How did you find the cure to cancer and other disease? How did you solve all the economic issues, and how did the world enter another war?" Jim asked each question with anger and frustration.

Shaun breathed deeply and continued to smile. "Jim, you ask too many questions. Why can't you just accept the fact that this is how it's all going to come down? I will answer one of your questions. This one is a given. The world bickered and complained. It became so angry and fed up with itself that everyone feared everyone else. Money and disease were the hot topics of the world. Each time someone claimed he would do something, he failed to provide a definitive solution.

"Eventually, the people were full of fear and discontent, to the point that they feared themselves. They begged their governments for a new kind of security. The world then split itself into ten different sections and raised arms against each other. This so-called security system was supposed to be fool-proof; that is, until one day people vanished. Chaos spread among the masses as the world nearly annihilated itself. Cities were decimated to ash, and nearly everyone was lost.

"My master said it was time to take action and release a new kind of technology that would be the catalyst for everything you see here today. I suppose this moment has occurred several times over. I sat here at my desk and had a video conference with you today, but we have had this exact conversation several times over. I have seen both sides of the future, Jim—one with you and one without you. I am giving you the opportunity to choose which side you want to be on. Should you choose to work with me, which I highly recommend, I will tell you where and when to go. When you arrive at the destination, you will have no more financial worries. You will be taken care of fully. So tell me, Jim, are you prepared to help create this world once again?"

Jim breathed in more deeply and at a faster rate. "You know, Shaun, I have seen you, and I know you for what you truly are. I don't know what kind of game you are trying to play, but I will not have any part of this."

Immediately, Shaun jumped up and shot back at Jim, "Whoa, whoa, whoa, Jim! What are you talking about?"

"Shaun, this is no game to me. This is reality. I spoke with God as well as Jesus today. I know they are real, and for all I know, this is not real; it's just some stupid dream or stupid trick."

Shaun's face became serious and his body tensed up. "What do you know about God, huh? Your God is dead. Do you really want me to believe that God would let innocent, good-hearted, and loving people die every day, by other people and disease? He is dead. Dead, dead, dead. I suppose I was a fool to think you would have said yes to a better life. It really does not matter, Jim; either way you look at it, the clock is ticking down. Should you decide, find me in two and a half years. I will be waiting for you in the field where you used to play. In the meantime don't bother looking for me; you will not find me. Should I want to find you—or anyone else, for that matter—I will do so as I please."

Jim rose to his feet with his fists clenched tightly and stormed toward the flat screen. Filled with anger, he gritted his teeth and then said, "Now, you listen to me. I know who you are, and I swear that I will stop you."

Shaun laughed hysterically. "Jim, you said you met with God and Jesus. If that is the truth, which I highly doubt, then you should realize that there is nothing you can do. What is it they say? What is written is what is said. There is one thing though, Jim—regardless of what you decide, we win." Shaun snapped his head and looked at Richard. "Richard, take him back."

"As you desire, sir," Richard responded loyally.

"Wait, you son of a—" Before Jim could finish his sentence, Richard knocked him flat on his back. Richard just glared at Jim and chuckled as he placed his fingertips in Jim's sternum and pressed deeply. Jim felt as if his ribs were breaking. Snapping sounds, like a twig, came from the center of Jim's chest where Richard was pressing. Richard then placed his other hand on Jim's sternum and applied an equal amount of pressure.

Jim felt paralyzed, to the point that he could not breathe. He began to choke as his body tensed up. A feeling of emptiness, like a black-hole, sucked at Jim from the top of his stomach where Richard's palm lay. Jim began to flail and convulse, as if he was having a seizure.

Richard grinned and replied, "Go!"

With a flicker, Jim was gone.

16

Jim awoke to a man in his mid-sixties shaking him. The elderly man wore an off-white suit, a bow tie, and a summer hat. Jim was lying on his back, as if he had slipped on a wet floor and passed out.

"Oh, thank goodness you are all right. I thought maybe you had died or something. I know you feel a bit groggy, but that is to be expected when you hit your head. I am a doctor. Can you open your eyes?"

Jim felt like he had been hit by a train. His head was throbbing fiercely, and his body ached all over. He squinted his eyes to shield them from the light. He attempted to lift himself, but the doctor forced him to lie down.

"Nope, not yet, sonny. First I want to do a little test to make sure you are going to be fine. I know you may be in some pain, but I am going to test your reflexes. I want you to follow my finger without moving your head." Jim nodded slightly. The doctor raised his index finger eight inches from Jim's face. He moved his finger from left to right and then up and down. "Now I am going to do the same test with a flashlight."

Once again, Jim slightly nodded. The doctor clicked on the flashlight and shone the light on the sides of Jim's eyes. The doctor nodded as he concluded this test. "All right, sonny, I'm going to help you up. If you need to sit down, just say so." The doctor assisted Jim very slowly to his feet. He placed Jim against the edge of the counter for added support and then checked Jim for any bruising or bumps on the back of his head. "My name is Alan Malone," the doctor said. "I work in a family practice in Memphis, Tennessee. It's been a long while since I've taken a vacation, and I was hoping to relax. As a doctor, though, I always must be on the alert and rightfully so."

"My name is Jim Ackelson. It's also been a while since I've taken a vacation. Now I'm not so certain that it was a good thing."

"I don't see anything wrong. I must advise you to be careful, since a storm is brewing out there. I didn't see any water spills on the floor, but maybe you lost your balance when the ship turned or something."

"I wonder—how long have I been out? Did you see a man in here wearing a tuxedo and sunglasses, with a nametag that read 'Richard'?"

Alan looked down at his watch and replied, "Nope, sonny, I don't remember seeing anyone of that nature. I just walked in here and saw you lying on the floor. It's currently seven in the evening and is getting pretty dark because of the storm."

Jim closed his eyes tightly. "So you mean that I have been lying here for nearly five hours, and nobody noticed me on the floor?"

Alan looked at Jim with great concern and placed his hand on Jim's shoulder. "Son, have you been drinking?"

Jim looked appalled and shook his head. "Alan, I appreciate all that you have done for me, but I really must get going." Jim abruptly left the restroom and went back to his room. He was lost in his thoughts and forgot about hunger and the food that he ordered.

Jim rushed past other passengers as he attempted to piece reality and fantasy together. Sweating profusely, Jim thought, *God what am I doing? Is this real or what? Could you please just give me a sign as to what I'm supposed to do?* The ship began to rock fiercely. Jim felt seasick and staggered like a drunken person. Heaving, Jim clutched his stomach and rushed to get to the elevator. People were swaying and holding on to handrails for support. A little girl's voice cried in the distant. "Daddy, I'm scared. Why is this happening?"

Jim was desperate for a breath of fresh air; it was difficult for him to breathe. The ship continued rocking, and Jim stumbled to a nearby door with an exit sign over it. Jim flung the door open, and the air pressure pulled Jim outside.

There were no stars or light, other than the dim lighting of the ship. The storm was great, as the wall of the waves extended in rolls of fifteen feet on either side. The clouds dispersed a torrential rain and were catapulted at great speeds by the wind. The rain stung Jim's exposed skin and drenched him. He heard cries from inside the ship, and someone called out, "Quick! Somebody help! That man is outside and is surely going to die unless we help!"

A wave slammed against the side of the ship. Jim held for dear life as the roaring waves slammed against him and into the ship. Once again, Jim felt like he had been hit by a train. Jim cried out, "God, have you brought me this far only to abandon me and let me die?"

God replied to Jim like the sound of thunder and with a crackling of lightning, "Jim, I love you and will never forsake you. Even though you have blatantly ignored what I have told you, I love you still." Crackling and thunder continued as the storm raged. "You have brought this rage of the sea against you and the ship. You should have trusted me and gone to Venezuela. Fall into the sea. I will bring you to where you are needed."

Jim began to cry again and replied, "God, forgive me, but I just don't want to die. How will I live if I fall into the sea?"

There was another fierce crackle as God replied, "Trust your life with me. I gave it to you."

Another wave slammed Jim against the side of the ship. A crew of employees rushed to the door; one held a life preserver. They just reached the door just as Jim allowed himself to be pulled into the sea by the retracting wave. Jim was tossed twenty feet away from the ship. He heard whistles blaring and a call of "Man overboard! Port side!" Jim tried swimming with all his might to stay afloat. He saw a man throw a life preserver with an attached rope at him. The waves rolled and drew Jim several hundred feet from the ship.

Even though he knew, deep in his heart, that God had just spoken to him, his faith that God would save him withered away. He inhaled deeply and thought all hope was lost. Just as he began to sink into the dark sea, the storm came to a halt. The clouds parted in the sky, and the stars shone brightly as they glistened off the calm ocean. Salt water poured into Jim's mouth any time that he tried to speak. A deep vibration covered him.

Something enormous lifted Jim. He felt like he was being carried but only just for a moment. He turned his head to see several thousand teeth and a long tongue. "Are you serious, God? This can't be happening to me. A friggin' whale is about to eat me?" Fear flooded his mind. Jim paddled as fast as he could away from the whale, but the whale closed its mouth over Jim, swallowed him, and dove back into the ocean.

17

Days were spent in darkness and in water. Jim's only priority was staying afloat and alive. That desire was followed by weariness and hunger. Time was irrelevant in this belly of the beast; there was no way to tell time. Jim could think only of surviving. His eyes adjusted to the darkness, and his senses grew stronger and allowed him to find random fish that the whale swallowed. Jim found a few planks of wood. He tore strips of clothing apart and tied them to the wood to create a makeshift floatation device. An occasional fish would bump into Jim's legs or arms, and he would eat it raw. He would bite into the scales on the sides of the fish, and blood and guts would ooze out. The dead fish were only part of the unpleasant smell.

Fatigued and hungry, this was an all-time low in Jim's life. His predicament made him sob throughout the day. "Why, God? Why have you forsaken me?" he cried. Jim ached all over from the lack of proper rest. "God, just let me die. I don't want to be digested alive. This place is terrible and very lonesome. For whatever I did to anger you, I am sorry. Just please get me the heck out of here!" Soon, Jim came to the breaking point and began blacking out at various times.

He was too tired to scream or to move, and death seemed imminent. In the little time that Jim was conscious, he spoke aloud to God, asking numerous questions about his past and whether he would die. The horrendous smell from decaying fish was atrocious.

The whale occasionally bellowed deep sounds that would vibrate its stomach slightly. At times, the bellowing gave Jim a mild headache. Jim no longer cared about anything—not his life back home, not getting hired, not even the pesky bill collectors. Jim was too exhausted to care about these things; all he wanted to do was to get out of the whale's belly alive. It did not matter to Jim whether his eyes were open or shut. Darkness surrounded him with no chance to escape.

Jim wondered if talking to himself was a sign of insanity. Then a person appeared in front of him, standing on the water. Even in darkness, Jim could see this individual as clear as day.

I must be delirious, Jim thought. The person that stood in front of him constantly changed appearances each time Jim blinked. The individual would be a six-foot-five linebacker for professional football team in one moment, and then he would be a five-foot-three Hispanic woman in the next. Within a few minutes, the person seemed to transfigure into both male and female of every ethnicity in the world.

Jim laughed hysterically but then stopped laughing completely as he croaked, "Who are you?"

The figure standing in front of Jim radiated light. Within seconds, the entire cavity of the whale's stomach was encompassed by pure, radiating light. Jim tucked his chin to his collarbone and tightly closed his eyes.

Gritting his teeth and moaning with pain, Jim placed his arms in front of his face to shield his eyes from the light. "For the love of God, please stop!" cried Jim.

"There is no pain. Open your eyes," replied the being.

Jim replied angrily, "My eyes were practically on fire. Pain shot to the back of my head and to my stomach. Who are you?"

"Be at peace. I am known by many names. I was with the Father and Jesus from the beginning. I am the one who was promised to come. I have come. I am the Comforter and have a direct connection with mankind and God. I am the Holy Spirit of God."

Exhaustion had taken its toll on Jim's body. He was too tired to argue with this entity. He opened his mouth to speak but closed it as he contemplated what to say to the Holy Spirit. "Am I going to die here?" asked Jim.

"No. You will not die here, nor shall you experience death. You are here because of your actions of disobedience. God has a set purpose for you and ensures your life."

Jim opened his eyes without pain, and still the Holy Spirit emitted the same light. A few planks of lumber floated across the top of the water and were surrounded by fish swimming around. "I know I screwed up. I know that I should have just trusted in God. What is so important in going to Venezuela? Could you at least tell me how long I have been here?"

"Jim, you have been here two days."

"Two days! You have got to be kidding me. This time has felt like eternity, and it has only been two days? There is simply no way, especially with how exhausted I am."

"I assure you, it has been only two days. Your mind has tricked you. Time, after all, is only an illusion and defined by mankind. I have come to minister the gospel of Jesus Christ to you. I am also here to strengthen your spiritual mind. You are without any influence and therefore, you are able to concentrate to a greater degree. Your spirit man resides near the upper part of your stomach and is able to receive the word more efficiently. I shall be here for a while and then return to my task. You will speak in new tongues when I leave and have a new foundation and understanding."

Jim took in what the Holy Spirit had to say and asked with a great measure of concern, "Tell me, how can I concentrate when I am so hungry? What is so important that I have to go to South America?"

"God has directed me to come here at this time. He told me to call out to you and bring you to the sea. God called the whale to swallow you and take you to South America. You will meet an evangelist named Pete Garcia. He will find you washed ashore and take you to the village where he lives. God called him to be an evangelist a year ago and called him to Venezuela. Although things are occurring there, do not worry; place your faith in God. Pete's village is the same village as was in your dream. The village has highly possessed people that God wishes to remove. Take up the full armor of God, for the man that you dream of is there, and Satan resides within him. Fear not of this, for it is only a part that must come to pass. God wants Jesus to return soon, but his children continually prevent him from doing so," explained the Holy Spirit.

"Whoa, whoa, whoa—wait a minute here. You have to understand that this is a whole lot of information to take in at once. I thought God was supposed to be almighty and powerful, so how is it that he can't have Jesus return any time that he wants to?"

"That is simple. Before God gave the law to mankind, sin resided on the earth. Mankind disregarded the law and sought evil ways. Mankind hid from God and turned to darkness. God looked onto the earth and saw filth and disgust. God felt agony that his beloved creation would turn away. He washed the earth to cleanse and purge it of the evil and disgust. The earth repopulated and turned toward darkness once more. Remembering his promise, God sent himself in human form to abide under the law and to make the greatest sacrifice that would amend mankind's evil ways.

"With his sacrifice, he completed the law and bridged the gap between him and mankind. You know this story, for it is the story of Jesus. Once Jesus died and rose again, he went to the Father and asked God to love his creation as he loved Jesus. Since no one would fit the criteria set by God to enter heaven, Jesus asked God to see the world through him. Now, when God looks on the world, he sees it through the blood of Jesus. This is why mercy and grace flow throughout the world."

"The Gentiles and the ones whose names are written in the Lamb's Book of Life pleaded with God not to allow the return of the King of Kings. They followed after selfish ambitions and not after the will of God. He wishes to end these sufferings and is coming soon. God has the ability and power to do anything he desires, but out of love, he hears his people and confides in Christ when answering. He confides in Christ because of his sacrifice. Instead of issuing wrath, Jesus pleads to give love."

"This is just ... wow. I don't know how this all can be," Jim said. "It's definitely unexpected truth and feels a bit above my pay grade, don't you think?"

"Jim, you could not be more wrong. God wishes these things to be known. People die from a lack of knowledge. If they were to actually seek God, I would be there to give them insight and knowledge of these things. Mankind is still foolish in these things. You must walk with love and selflessness, get in the Word, and meditate throughout the day. Your spiritual ears will develop, and you will hear me speaking to you with a soft voice, but it will be as clear as day. The time has arrived. You are about to fall into a deep sleep to allow for a safe passage to the shoreline. Sleep."

Immediately, Jim's eyelids closed, and his breathing went into a rhythm.

The Holy Spirit retracted its light and disappeared. The whale moaned and began violently twisting and turning. A deep bellow came from beyond the stomach of the whale. A rush of wind pushed Jim forward to the teeth of the whale. The whale continued to act in a violent motion, and then its jaws opened. Water flowed above the whale's teeth and into the ocean. Jim floated down on his makeshift raft, out of the whale's mouth, moving toward the shoreline. The whale submerged and departed, and Jim continued to float until he was washed up on the shore.

18

Jim awoke to the sound of waves rolling onto the shoreline and seagulls squawking overhead. The sun beat down on Jim's back. He extended his fingers and then clenched them. He grabbed a fistful of sand and mud. Jim opened his eyes slowly to avoid getting sand blown into his eyes. A seagull walked just two feet from where Jim lay. Jim thought the bird seemed almost tame, and it dawned on him that he must be near civilization—that would explain why the seagull didn't seem afraid of him.

Jim's skin was cold and clammy in some areas and hot and itchy in others. Jim's clothes, skin, and hair were covered in sand. *How long have I been here?* Jim thought. His vision went in and out of focus for the next several minutes. Finally, he noticed a variety of trees several yards from where he lay. A man was shouting near the edge of the trees. Several people walked out from the trees, but Jim could not tell how many people there were in the group.

Most of the people looked somewhat civilized. Most were men in worn dress shirt, pants, and sandals. A few women were in the group, but Jim could not see them clearly. Jim coughed deeply and tightened his core while doing so. He attempted to crawl but his efforts were in vain. He felt paralyzed, as if all his strength had left him. The group from the forest were running to Jim and shouting at him. Jim blinked twice … and fell back asleep.

Jim awoke as the group of people was placing him on top of a bamboo stretcher. He was in a daze, and his head was spinning and throbbing. He closed his eyes as several men picked him up and carried him away. He awoke some time later to a musky and dimly lit room. His back was sore, but his entire body ached as though he had been beaten.

A few sun rays pierced through random cracks in the wall. Jim rubbed his eyelids and then his face. He ran his hands down his body to ensure that he was in the same condition as when he left. His face was as rough as sandpaper from the stubble of facial hair. His clothes were more rough and tattered than what Jim remembered. He lifted the blanket above his body to find that he had a change of clothes. Jim blushed, feeling embarrassed as he thought, *Boy, I hope they didn't look at anything.*

His eyes adapted to the lighting of the room, which he saw held only a bed and a chair. Jim was hungry and was curious to learn how long he had been out. His head still throbbed with a headache. Jim sat up and planted his feet on the floor. He slowly stood up and walked to the door. When he opened the door, blinding sunlight spilled into the room, and Jim closed his eyes and blinked until his eyes were somewhat adjusted. After a few stumbling steps, he successfully made it outside on to the dirt road.

Jim kept his head down and his eyes on the ground, which was blanketed with reddish-brown dirt. "*Hola, señor,*" said someone in front of Jim.

Confused, Jim replied, "Sir, I don't speak Spanish."

Pete replied in a mild accent, "Oh, so I take it you are an American. Hello, sir, I am Pete Garcia, and I am an evangelist. God sent me here to this village. He told me that his Word needed to be spread. This village is polluted with many spirits, demons, and devils who have taken a stronghold here; some have taken residence in the villagers here. Come with me to my house for some breakfast and so that we may talk."

Pete placed Jim's arm around his shoulder and assisted him to his house. The house was not too much bigger than the place where Jim had been. The floor was made of cement, and the walls were bare. Pete took Jim to an office. A bookcase was half full with a variety of books. A desk and three chairs were centered in the room. Pete placed Jim in a chair facing a window, and then Pete sat at the desk. Dust particles floated in the room and were made visible by the sun rays that lit up Pete's desk.

Pete called in a loud voice, "*Señora Gabriela, venga aquí, por favor.*"

A lady entered the room from behind Jim and Pete. "*Sí, señor,*" replied Gabriela.

"*Por favor, haga algo para comer. Mi amigo tiene mucho hambre.*"

"*Ah, sí señor. ¿Qué quieres comer?*" replied Gabriela.

"*Dos huevos, tocino, frijoles y tortillas con un vaso de agua, por favor.*"

"*Sí señor, es no problema,*" replied Gabriela with a smile. She turned and left the room.

"Uh, Pete, what did you just say?" Jim asked.

"I told her to bring you breakfast—two eggs, bacon, beans, and tortillas with a glass of water."

"I'm sorry 'bout that, Pete. I should have learned to speak another language, but I really didn't think I would ever use it. It would have made a world of a difference now."

"So tell me, Jim … I know that God has a purpose for you here in this village. He has told me this among many great secrets. Tell me a little about yourself and how you came to be washed up on shore."

"Well, it's a really crazy story really. I was taken to heaven and saw the creation and downfall of man, as well as the fall of Lucifer. God instructed me to come here, but I was disobedient. I got a free cruise ticket from my grandmother for my birthday. It would have cost all that was in my bank account, which wasn't much, to get a ticket down here. Instead, I took the free one and got on a cruise liner to Jamaica.

"While on the ship, the Antichrist made an offer to me, but I declined. I tried to go back to my room, but a crazy storm broke out because of me. I had the strongest desire to go outside. It was there that the Holy Spirit told me to let myself fall into the ocean. A friggin' whale swallowed me and had me in his belly for about three days. The Holy Spirit dropped by and decided it was time to have a little chat. It caused me to fall into a deep sleep, from which I awoke while on the beach. The next thing I knew was that I was in an unfamiliar room with unfamiliar clothes. I barely had the strength to walk outside, but then I ran into you. I would say that about sums it up."

Pete looked with awe at Jim. "Wow, it sounds like you have had quite the adventure lately. I suppose that you will go through a great deal more. God has told me in my spirit to expect you. He told me that you would be there on the beach and that I was to get you and bring you back here. He said that you are in need of a mentor, teacher, and friend. He said that I was to teach you all that I know in the wisdom and truth of God. The times are growing closer, for we are near the return of our King. God has told me that we are in turmoil and have entered into the period of time of the great falling away of the faithful. Those not rooted in their faith shall fall away from God. Jim, the world is about to endure the greatest of hardships, and it shall test them to the core of their faiths. This is why the return of our King is so close."

"Pete, that sounds pretty scary. I have a question for you. While speaking with the Holy Spirit, he said time was irrelevant. What exactly did he mean by that?" asked Jim.

"I have been meditating and asking God about that," Pete said. "I have asked why it takes God a while to answer some people's prayers. He explained this mystery to me. Imagine God as the center or the beginning and the end of time—"

"How can God be the beginning and the end of time?" Jim interrupted.

Before anything, including time, God was there," Pete explained. "Time is irrelevant, as it is measured by mankind's laws and rules. God is not bound by these mediocre things. Like I said, imagine God as the beginning and the end and as light. When he began creating, he went forward and shot out into the distance. God eventually got to a point and turned. He turned enough that eventually, he would return to himself, as if creating a gigantic circle. There, he could look at himself and see the things he had done and the things that had and would occur. This is why a day for us is a thousand years to God and vice versa. It is not that it took a thousand years for God to return to himself. Albert Einstein understood this concept and created his equation for the speed of light, which in turn aided him in his theory of relativity. We, as humans, attempt to measure how God moves or works, but it is irrelevant, because God decides the precise moment to create."

Gabriella entered the room with a wooden platter holding the food Pete had requested, along with silverware and a folded cloth napkin. She placed the platter in front of Jim with a smile.

"*Gracias*, Gabriella," said Pete.

"Thank you," said Jim.

"*De nada*," replied Gabriella, and she left the room in a quiet manner.

Pete gestured to the food, telling Jim, "Go ahead, Jim; dig in." Pete continued to talk while Jim ate. "I don't know if you know, Jim, but there are many evil things in the world. Have you ever thought of where all the demons and evil spirits went? If you read the Word, you know that Jesus healed the sick and rid people of demons, devils, and evil spirits. How is it that today in the world, they are nonexistent?"

Jim had his mouth full of tortillas and eggs, so he simply shook his head.

"Well, you see, Jim," Pete said, "the Devil has gone to great depths to fool the world. He has done all that he can do to make people believe that there is no God and no Devil, no heaven or hell, and especially no demons, devils, or spirits. I tell you that demons, devils, and spirits are out and about more than ever. The world is full of them. Another thing the Devil has done is made Christians believe that they are powerless. They do not know their biblical rights, and they do not know to use the Word of God.

"If they knew what power we are to exercise, Jesus would have returned by now. Did you know that we are supposed to be out preaching the gospel, healing the sick, and removing the demons, devils, and spirits from people? We have the ability to even raise the dead. Jesus said that doing all these things would be evidence of him within us. Satan has struck fear within our hearts and has done this for the lack of faith. Again I tell you, Jim, that time, although irrelevant, is short. Come with me; it is time to begin your training, for this mystery man is coming. He is not something to be feared, but you still need the Word to be steadfast within you. The Word is the only way that you are going to overcome the task to come." Pete stood, and as he did, he looked ready for war. He helped Jim to his feet, and together, they left the room.

19

Pete took Jim behind his house. The ground was bare with a few patches of grass and weeds. "Jim, you are considered to be a child. That's not in a literal aspect—you have some knowledge of the Word, but it will not help you battle the kingdom of darkness. I believe that this is one of the reasons why God chose you to come to this village. I have studied the Scriptures for several decades now. In light of this, I have grown in a strong walk and fellowship with God and Christ. I used to practice religion, but God gave me a revelation one night. The Holy Spirit came to me in a dream and told me to depart from my ways. He said that practicing old ways of tradition would only hinder and separate an actual walk and fellowship. So I decided to set out like Jesus did, and I went into the wilderness."

Jim's mouth dropped open in awe. "Do you mean to tell me that you were following what everyone else did?" he asked. "Did you go into the wilderness without any supplies and for forty days?"

Pete smiled. "Initially, I was excited, but I was also full of fear. I really didn't know what to expect. I treated it like a vacation, thought I had no idea how long I would be gone. I simply felt led by the spirit to go, so I went. I went with a pen, my Bible, a couple changes of clothes—mainly socks and underwear—and a sleeping bag. I figured that I would leave the rest for God to take care of. I went walking until I eventually left civilization altogether. I was alone, with the Word in my hand and my heart. My body and soul were left open for God to shape and mold me. I can tell you that the first two weeks were the roughest."

"Why exactly were the first two weeks the hardest?" Jim asked. "Did Satan tempt you like Jesus? What hardships did you encounter?"

Pete smiled again and answered, "I never visually saw Satan, but I did feel the spirit of temptation on a constant basis. I felt conflicted between my flesh and my spirit man. They were pulling me in different directions. God provided food and water; it was kind of like Basic Survival 101. I found food at the exact moment when I needed it, and it was the same with water. Eventually, my body was ratified and cleansed from impurities. This allowed me to ingest what God wanted me to hear. On the night of the seventh day of week two, my body had a fit as I developed a fever. I was drenched in sweat, and my body began convulsing. The Lord said that my body was finally conforming to the Spirit, and the unclean spirits that were oppressing me were being forced out.

"I eventually passed out from the amount of energy that it drained from me. At four in the morning, I awoke to the Holy Spirit walking near me. I saw more angels than I could count looking at me. A voice called down from the heavens and said, 'My people die because they have a lack of knowledge. My people have fallen away from me, away from the straight and narrow. I tell you that this is the period of the great falling away.' The voice left me speechless and in tears."

Pete stared at the ground as tears formed in his eyes. "I simply could not stand. I wept like a baby because I felt so unworthy."

Jim knew this feeling all too well. He'd felt the same way when he encountered Jesus in heaven. "Pete, I know how you feel. I know that I was sent here to do a work for God. If I am a child and you are my spiritual advisor, then please let's get started with this training."

Pete nodded and replied, "You are absolutely correct. The time is short, and God definitely has a work for you to accomplish here. The first thing we must accomplish is the basics. We are going to cover reading the Word, praying over the Word, and rereading the Word. We are going to fast for a week and meditate on the Word. I don't know how long this is going to take, but I am sure God will see us through."

For nine months, Pete and Jim read the Word, prayed, and occasionally fasted. Jim gained a significant amount of knowledge of the Word and a newfound relationship with God. The Holy Spirit visited Jim on numerous occasions. The Holy Spirit led Jim and Pete to different people at various times. Jim and Pete were instructed to bring and anoint a canister of olive oil. The people to whom they were led were full of nonviolent, unclean spirits, demons, and devils. Pete always stood behind the individual and translated for Jim whenever there was an exchange of language. Pete placed his hands on the shoulders of the individual. Jim instructed the individual to focus his mind on God.

For several weeks, Pete and Jim went about casting out spirits, demons, and devils. Each night, they would come together and have intense prayer meetings. During these meetings, they would pray only in their holy spiritual language. On the fourth night, about 3:30 a.m., Pete had a vision. The vision showed both him and Jim approaching a man who was considered to be an outcast and of the lowest caste in society. He was considered crazy and unable to hold a conversation. He would babble and rant and rave in Spanish. He did not know any other language. He was filthy and was sick with a skin disease, as well as other diseases. This man lived a full day's walk outside of the village.

The next morning, Pete woke up and had a stirring in his body with his spirit man. He knew that he and Jim were going to go find this man. After he woke up Jim, Pete explained his vision to him and said that he knew the area to look for the man.

They walked to the edge of the village and gave praise to God and Jesus for this day. They then thanked God for revealing where to go. Within seconds of their praise and thanksgiving, the Holy Spirit gave them the direction to find this man. They walked through the nearby forest and through the thick brush. The birds chirped as serpents slivered through the underbrush. Several insects buzzed near their heads. Their shirts were drenched in sweat by the time they came to a small opening. They observed a makeshift roof and sleeping quarters. Shade covered the area and made it difficult to see inside the sleeping quarters.

Pete glanced in the area but found no one inside. "He has to be here somewhere," said Pete. They split up and searched on opposite sides of the area.

Jim called loudly, "Call out if you see him." Jim inhaled deeply and slowly exhaled as he thought, *Where are you?* Jim scanned the area and saw several trees as well as the underbrush. He saw something moving slowly in the distance. "Hey, Pete, I think I got something over here," called Jim.

Pete ran excitedly toward Jim. They approached the thing that was moving, wondering if it was a crippled animal. They continued moving closer and soon realized it was the man they were looking seeking. The man growled at them like a jaguar. His clothes were tattered, and his hair was wild. They approached the man boldly and without fear. They knew they had put on the full armor of God this day and knew where their authority lay.

Jim prayed over the canister of olive oil. He unscrewed the cap, placed his finger over the opening of the bottle, and tipped the bottle to allow the anointed oil to flow onto his finger. Jim then traced a small cross on the man's forehead with the oil on his finger. Jim placed his palm on the man's forehead, with his other hand reaching toward heaven. "Pete, let's begin," said Jim.

Both simultaneously closed their eyes and began speaking in an unknown and holy language, which was God's holy language.

For several minutes, the man they were praying over convulsed. Jim said in an authoritative voice, "Depart from this vessel, you unclean and evil spirits." The man began making a grotesque choking and sucking noise. His teeth were grinding together as his body tensed up. His neck turned several degrees and popped. His stomach contracted, and the man began to heave as though he was about to puke. He then laughed hysterically and began to question Jim. "Exactly who do you think you are? Who are you to tell me what to do? We live here and like it here."

Jim was taken aback and felt confused. He didn't know what to say. Every time he prayed over people and cast them out, they never fired back at him. All the spirits left without hesitation.

Jim tried to outsmart the spirits and replied, "You can't remain in this body. You have to leave immediately. Now get out!"

The man shook his head and shouted, "You have no authority and can't tell us what to do!"

Jim felt fear in the pit of his stomach. Pete continued praying in tongues. The Holy Spirit reminded Jim of the truth.

Jim replied once more to this man, "I am speaking to you under the authority of Jesus Christ of Nazareth. He has charged me to cast you out."

The unclean spirits knew what was about to happen. They tried to reason with Jim and fill him with doubt by saying, "It is all a lie. You can't—"

"Be quiet!" Jim said angrily. At that moment, it was as though someone had stapled the man's lips together. Jim continued, "By the authority that Jesus Christ gave us, the living Word of God says that what I bind here on earth will be bound in heaven, and whatever I loose here on earth will be loosed in heaven. Unclean spirits, I bind all of you up. I call you defeated and command you to depart. You don't belong here, for he belongs to Christ. I command you by the precious blood and in the name of Jesus to depart immediately."

The man blacked out and fell backward against Pete's palms. Pete slowly lowered the man to the ground and continued praying in his holy language.

Jim smiled at Pete and said, "I saw three unclean spirits break up and flee in different directions."

The man's skin was similar to the scales of a reptile. As the spirits fled from the man's body, the scales flaked from his skin and fell to the ground. Within seconds, the man had no visible ailments. He was physically and spiritually liberated. Pete and Jim always waited until the individual woke up and then they gave instructions on how to remain spiritually free. The individuals always woke with a smile and said they felt liberated.

Pete and Jim continued casting out unclean spirits, demons, and devils throughout the village until everyone was liberated.

20

few days had passed since they'd liberated the man in the forest. It was dusk as Pete approached Jim and shook his hand. "I want to thank you for all that you have done. You have been a true blessing and a good friend I am happy to call brother. We have gone through a great deal of training and situations. I have a warning to tell you, though. I received a phone call from another evangelist from a few villages farther north. It seems that there is a man coming this way. He seems to have a trail of sickness and possessions following him. I'm not sure, but it sounds to me like this may be the guy you have been talking about."

Jim dropped his smile when he heard this. "I suppose the time you mentioned has finally come upon us. I need a minute. I am going to take a walk to clear my head and to meditate on what I need to do," replied Jim. Pete nodded and left Jim to his thoughts.

Jim stuck both hands in his pockets and stared at the ground as he walked into the forest. As he walked, he thought about how to approach the situation. Jim came to a clearing in the forest, and he looked at the sky as he began speaking aloud. "God, I know that I have had some rough times, but I also know that you have been with me the entire time. This is going to be a whole different ball game. I suppose that after all of my training and practical use of your Word that this should be nothing different. I suppose that I am scared that I am going to fail miserably. I just want to thank you for all that you have done and are going to do. Regardless of what happens, praise be to your name and praise to the King of Kings."

The clouds began to swirl like they were being sucked into a vacuum. They spun faster and faster until they dispersed. A crackle and pop came from above as a lightning bolt struck a bush a few yards from where Jim was standing. Jim jumped back, full of fear. The bush became engulfed with flames but there was no smoke.

A voice spoke from the bush, "I am the great I am. Be not of fear, for I have not given mankind the spirit of fear. I have given you the spirit of wisdom and love. You have done well with training and praise. I am well pleased with you, Jim, but still your task is at hand. You have nothing to fear with the man that is coming. Go to this village's warehouse in two days. It is located on the southern outskirts of town. Do not enter the building until 12:33 a.m. Satan has taken hold of the man inside, just as he took hold of Judas Iscariot. I have told Satan to be inside the warehouse at the appointed time. Although it is unclear to you at this time, the time has come, and it must come. Fear not, but take up my full armor. Remember my Word when he lashes at you, for it is written on your heart. Even after you have completed these things, there is a great deal to do in the world. You shall be accompanied by James and Kyle to save George. You must now return to your current residence and in prayer through my holy language."

The flames on the bush shot into the sky and was carried away by a gust of wind. Amazed and excited by what he had just seen and heard, Jim ran all the way home. He passed several people who were laughing and dancing. The village was full of joy and love. Jim sprinted to the front door, and because he was running too fast, he stumbled as he tried to slow down and slammed right into the door, ricocheting off it like a rubber ball. He landed on his butt and bounced a couple of times before he returned to his feet. He dusted off his pants and decided to enter the house like a civilized person.

Gabriella opened the door curiously while looking to see who caused the noise. She saw Jim and smiled. Jim nodded his head and entered the house, where he met Pete on his way to his room. "Pete, you aren't gonna believe this."

Pete chuckled and replied, "Jim, you have some of the wildest stories. I'm sure that I can pretty much handle anything you tell me. So tell me, what happened this time?"

Jim chuckled and replied, "When I left here earlier, I eventually walked through the forest and found a small clearing. I looked up to the sky and began talking to God. I eventually got to thanking and praising him when the clouds began swirling. They then dispersed, and a lightning bolt shot down and struck a bush, engulfing it in flames. Can you believe it? It happened just like it did in the Old Testament. God just started talking to me. I'm so excited for all the things he has done and is about to do."

"Amen to that, brother. You really do have interesting events. I'm thankful that God has crossed our paths," replied Pete.

Jim entered his room full of glee. He went to the dresser and took his Bible from the dresser. He sat down on his bed and flipped open to the book of Psalms. He read a couple of chapters and then felt the need to read Proverbs for some wisdom. Jim spent an hour reading and dissecting the Word. After a couple of verses, he would come to a stopping point and begin praying in tongues. Jim continued praying until he could pray no more and eventually, he fell asleep reading the Word. Jim spent the next two days preparing for the task at hand. He strengthened his spirit man by reading the Word. He knew that if he was ill prepared, he would certainly fall during the battle.

21

Jim arrived alone at 12:32 a.m. and waited as directed. He said a brief prayer. "Dear heavenly Father, I plead the precious blood of Jesus over me, from the tops of my head to the soles of my feet. I proclaim that no harm or pain shall come against me this day. I say that any weapon formed against me shall not prosper. I thank you for being with me and strengthening me. Be with me during the times that I am weak. I speak this in Jesus' precious name, amen."

Jim opened the door at 12:33. A few dim lights were scattered across from the ceiling. Jim took a few steps inside of the building to get a better look. The door had a hinged actuator attached at the top of the door and closed from the pressure; the door was surprisingly silent. Looking around inside the warehouse, Jim found only rusted steel support beams and a dust-covered floor—and a man wearing a beige trench coat, standing in the center of the warehouse. The man had his back to Jim and stood still, like he was staring at something. Jim could not fully make out the man's features.

Jim cautiously approached the man, trying to avoid making any noise, which would cost him the element of surprise. Jim was quite scared. His blood and adrenaline were pumping fast; his hands and feet pulsated. Jim held every other breath—he feared that his breathing and heartbeat were too noisy and would signal the man.

Each step felt like a thousand pounds of weight. Jim dreaded each step that brought him closer to this man. He thought of different scenarios—some where he would be killed and others where he was victorious. Each scenario led to another, and each filled Jim with fear. Jim thought, *Shut up, you stupid Devil. God has already told me that I am not going to die here. What do you know anyhow?*

Jim felt he was insane for coming here without a physical weapon. He pondered what he was supposed to do. The only instruction he had was to be here and not enter until 12:33. Jim continued to tread carefully and stopped when he was three feet away from the man.

"I suppose the time has come," the man said. He turned and looked at Jim, full of hatred. "So tell me, Jim, why have you come? Are you truly that ignorant to listen to a dead God? Do you not know who has all the power?"

"God is not dead. I was there when he threw your happy butt out of heaven. You were selfish from the get-go. All you desired was power for yourself. You have destroyed all that I have known or loved. I have dreamed of you since I can remember. I have dreamed of the one you sent to seize control on earth. Why must you continue this pile of crap of destruction when in the end, you lose?" asked Jim.

The man laughed hysterically. "Jim, you really ought to look at the bigger picture. How is it that I am the selfish one here? Have I ever demanded that anyone worship me? No. Have I ever demanded blood sacrifices? No. So how am I the bad guy here? You know this vessel has been dreaming of this encounter every night for the last six years. The sad thing is, he never gets to see the ending. Isn't that a terrible thing, to watch a movie over and over and never get to finish it?"

"I will defeat you, Satan. I do not know who that man is, but I know who you are," said Jim.

"Well, Jimmy boy, if you know who I am and you have done your research, you will know that I am God on this earth. I have been given the power and authority here. I will destroy you, and I will prove that God can be wrong. I will raise myself and dethrone him, for I am the true God and not a wash-up sham," replied Satan.

Jim laughed uncontrollably, which aggravated Satan, and he asked, "What is a pathetic excuse for a human like you laughing about?"

Still laughing, Jim replied, "If you had done your research, you would know that you have no authority over the blood of the Lamb. Jesus defeated you and gave us the authority over you and your kingdom. Now bend over, Satan, and prepare for a butt whuppin'."

Angry and frustrated, Satan responded, "*Enough*, you swine. Die!" The man disappeared and began laughing ominously all around Jim, as if he were circling him.

Every few seconds, Jim felt as if somebody grabbed his insides and squeezed with a death grip. Each time caused his lungs to constrict and his breathing to become difficult.

"I will kill you, Jim, you can bet your life on it," said Satan.

Angry, Jim lashed back, "Face me, you disgusting coward. I know what you really look like on the inside. God granted me the pleasure of seeing you stripped from glory to your hideous figure."

"Oh, so you think you can take me on full force? I tell you what; I will face you, but don't expect me to go easy on you. I intend to kill you, one of God's precious creations," Satan sneered.

Jim began praying aloud. "God, grant me sight to fully see what is occurring in the spiritual realm." Jim immediately felt an invisible veil lift from his eyes. The man appeared five feet in front of Jim. The man held his right arm parallel to the floor with his palms up. The man smiled deeply as a dark, staff manifested. The staff was glowing with a dark purplish color and was vibrating. Jim knew this must be a weapon of some kind.

The man smirked. "I hope you made amends for anything you may have done. It's time to die, Jimmy boy." The man raised his right arm fully and lunged forward. He swung downward with ease. His speed was unreal, and Jim was almost unable to sense it. At the last second, Jim stepped inches out of the path of the blade. Jim cocked his right arm and gave the man a right hook. The man was caught off guard and stumbled backwards. "You promised a butt whuppin'.

That punch may have affected this flesh a little bit but has done nothing to me. So tell me what you are going to do now?" Satan said.

Jim quickly thought of something to do that would inflict damage. He remembered what the Scripture had said about it not being a battle of the flesh but a battle of the spirit. He then remembered that he was to take up the armor of God—breastplate of righteousness, helmet of salvation, feet with the gospel of peace, belt of truth, shield of faith, and the sword of the Spirit, which is the Word of God.

He also remembered that the Word of God is sharper than a double-edged sword and was initially used by Jesus to defeat Satan. "You know what, Satan? I finally get it. I know why you are always so angry and take it out on everybody else. You are always upset because you don't have anyone to unconditionally love you. You also look uglier than ugly. I'm going to step on your ugly head. You are a triple "D"—a dumb, defeated Devil!"

Satan was infuriated now, but before he could do anything, Jim prayed again. "Father, I thank you that you have given me the strength and authority to overcome this monstrosity, amen." Jim pointed his right index finger at Satan. "Now listen here, you mangled and decrepit being. I promised you a butt whuppin', and you're going to get it. I'm going to overcome you, just like Jesus did initially. *Etu keetush ama teeleya nahsewah aluohn. Matae asho leekandu.*" Jim spoke in unknown tongues, the holy language. While he was praying aloud, a four-foot sword of flames manifested in Jim's hands. The man looked full of fear. He turned around and tried to run while squealing like a little girl.

Jim heard a voice say, "Let him have it." Jim spoke the name of Jesus aloud, raised his arm and then pulled it forward, and the sword extended into a whip. The whip slapped the guy on his back, throwing him to the floor. The man was temporarily paralyzed, which caused Satan to crawl out of the man. Satan was in the same form as Jim had seen. The same as when God stripped him of his righteousness. "Oh, no you don't," said Jim as he cocked his arm back to deliver another blow. Jim slapped Satan with the instrument in his hand, while calling Satan defeated by the blood of Jesus. Each time the whip slapped Satan's back, Satan felt like he was being hit by a million volts of electricity. Satan roared with agony with each blow. Jim continued beating Satan for nearly twenty minutes without ceasing.

"Depart from here, you foul and defeated beast. Away from me, you dumb, defeated Devil. In the precious blood of Jesus, I call you defeated. In the authority he has given me over you, I command you to leave!" Once Jim ceased speaking, Satan flew up to the ceiling.

Satan gave one last reply. "Still there are those of your friends that I can destroy. Too bad for you, especially since you can't be there to warn them. George is a man after my own heart. I will see you again, Jim—you can believe that." Satan departed with a treacherous and agonizing screech.

"Thank you, Father, for ending this ordeal," said Jim. The Holy Spirit appeared immediately in front of Jim. The Holy Spirit continued to change features with every look.

"Your time here is almost at an end. Wait three weeks before returning home. You will have an unexpected visitor, and you two will return home on foot. Your task is only half completed and will be completed with the three of your friends. Return to Pete and inform him of the man who is paralyzed on the floor. He will return to normal but will not remember anything of the spiritual warfare."

The Holy Spirit departed after delivering the message. Jim felt weak and tired, but he had a strong desire to kneel and worship the true and living God. Jim prayed ten minutes in the Spirit and, as usual, fell asleep from the strain of the spiritual realm.

22

A voice woke Jim when it called to him, saying, "Get up and go to Pete." Jim was a little startled but then was comforted and assured by the voice. The air was damp from humidity, and it was still dark outside. Jim felt energized from the nap he had taken. He felt a little guilty that he'd passed out due to exhaustion, but he knew the reason for it. Jim left the warehouse and walked back to Pete's house. When Pete answered Jim's knock on the door, Jim cried out, "Boy, do I have some awesome news to tell you! The Holy Spirit just told me to go to you. The battle is finished. Satan possessed a man but fled from him. I gave him a whuppin', that's for sure. With the first blow from the Word of God, the man fell to the ground, paralyzed. I was instructed to tell you about him. He is still there, passed out and paralyzed."

Without a word, Pete nodded and left his house immediately. Jim went to his room and fell asleep. He woke the next morning to the delicious smell of food cooking in the kitchen. He inhaled deeply and with a smile. When he went to the kitchen, Pete greeted him with a simple meal of tortillas and beans, which was gold in Jim's view—Jim loved tortillas and beans for any meal of the day.

"How did you sleep?" asked Pete.

"Man, I haven't slept that good in years. I suppose that it has a great deal to do with my clear conscience and my first task completed," replied Jim.

"I believe it is because you have been asleep for nearly three weeks now. Sit ... sit and enjoy. The Lord has revealed to me that your time here has come to an end."

"I've been asleep for three weeks?" Jim asked. "Really? That seems almost impossible. Was I in a coma?"

"No, I can't say you were in a coma. Believe it or not, you also sleepwalked to the bathroom. You also occasionally woke up in the middle of the night, screaming. You were screaming something about a guy named George," replied Pete.

Jim frowned and studied the wall behind Pete.

Pete stared at Jim and asked, "What is it? Is it something I said?"

Jim focused back on reality and replied, "George is one of my best friends. It's something that God said to me before my encounter with Satan. He said that my other two friends and I would save George. I wish sometimes that God would not talk in riddles but would flat out tell me what he wants and what is to come."

"Well, my friend, God speaks to us in the manner in which we are to take it. He gives us enough insight to endure to victory. Although he may speak in riddles, you must take it as a blessing. Many in the world are closed off from God. Some never understand, and some never hear his voice. You are among the select who have accepted the calling. For this, you must give praise. Give praise that your name is written in the Lamb's Book of Life and praise that he calls you his child."

Jim finished his meal, full and satisfied, and he meditated on what Pete said. Jim placed his plate and glass in the sink and turned to embrace Pete in a brotherly hug. "Thanks for everything, Pete. It's time for me to hit the road. I feel led in my spirit that the time has come as well. It's going be a heck of a time getting back, though. God said that I had to return on foot."

Pete smiled and replied, "Jim, you should not always take things like this in a negative perspective. God apparently wants you to go on foot for a reason. Just take it as a blessing in disguise. Remember what Jesus said in the gospel of Luke 12:24. 'Consider the ravens:

They do not sow or reap, they have no storeroom or barn: yet God feeds them.' And Luke 12:29 says, 'And do not set your heart on what you will eat or drink.' If God has you walking by foot, then he will, as always, take care of you."

They broke their embrace, and Pete followed Jim to the front door. Jim turned to Pete and said, "Please thank Gabriella for all she has done for me."

"I will be sure to do that. I will be praying for you, Jim. Stay in faith and walk with peace."

Jim walk outside but was stopped in his tracks. He smiled, chuckled and waved at two familiar men that stood in front of him—Asrel and James. Once they made eye contact, James ran towards Jim and bear-hugged him. Jim was knocked off balance and nearly fell to the floor. "I knew it! I friggin' knew it," said James.

Struggling to breathe, Jim broke free of James' grasp. Coughing, Jim replied, "I missed you too, but tell me what you knew? Where did you guys come from, and what are y'all doing here?"

James's expression changed to one of great concern as he asked, "Jim, you really don't know, do you?" When Jim simply shrugged, James explained, "Everyone thinks you're dead. You have been missing for near eleven months. They said you fell overboard, and they searched for a month for you. Something inside of me told me you were alive. I refused to believe you were dead, and I began talking to God. I asked him to give me a sign or something. It really is a long story and one that I believe will be better told while we walk."

Jim felt lost and confused. "Everyone thinks I'm dead? The Holy Spirit told me to fall into the sea. I was swallowed by a friggin' whale, just like Jonah. I have been here for a while, and boy, do I have some stories to tell you. What do you mean, 'while we walk'? How did you know I was going to walk back home?"

James chuckled. "It will be an interesting trek. I was told by the Holy Spirit that we are to leave immediately. He told me that I would join you in a walk back home. This walk is to strengthen our spirit men inside of us. The journey ahead is long and grueling, but as long as we labor in the Lord, it will be a blessing."

Jim then turned to Asrel. "So tell me: what part do you have to play in this?"

Asrel looked at Jim with the same calm, cool, and collected expression and replied, "I was to bring James here at this appointed time. I will not be accompanying you on your journey back home. Take refuge in the Lord and take hold of the armor of God. For without it, you will struggle to find victory. Only through Christ will you be able to succeed. Until then, Jim, may God lead your path."

A deep wind blew against James, Pete, and Jim. As the wind moved, Asrel departed with it. Jim turned to Pete and nodded and then began walking through the village.

The people smiled and waved at Jim and James. Jim felt accomplished and full of joy from relieving this town of the evil that had resided within the villagers.

"You must have done some work here, Jim. Everyone here looks full of Joy."

Jim looked at James and replied, "They are, James. The kingdom of darkness spread throughout this village and the world like a plague. God sent me here to alleviate the villagers of this and to remind them that he loves them and has not forgotten about them." Jim and James walked to the outskirts of the village. Jim stopped to look back at the village. He felt sad for leaving the village that had been his home for almost a year. "If I had only known then what I know about the love of God now, things would have been so much different. James, since we are about to depart, how about we say a quick prayer?"

James nodded at Jim and they joined hands. They both bowed their heads as Jim began the prayer. "Lord, you have been with us, through and through. Our journey is not finished yet but seemingly has only just begun. I ask that you be will us and mentor us as we begin our journey. Strengthen our spirit men as well as our flesh, that we may endure the works of Satan and his kingdom. May we fulfill your will and may the end come soon with the return of the King of Kings, amen."

Jim and James continued their trek, following dirt roads, while James explained his story.

Jim and James' journey continues in the second
book of this series, *Covert Glory.*